Jacob's

Bondage

Book one of:

Jacob's Struggle

By: Boris Copper

DEDICATION

This book is dedicated to Jacob Stall, the young boy who inspired it,
and to the fine members of *Notebored*, the online group who
gave the author so many valuable crits and encouragement.
Without them all, this story would never have been conceived let alone birthed.

ISBN: 0615953166
ISBN-13: 978-0615953168

CONTENTS

1 Kidnapped

Jacob was watching the *Jymstyne Pyrro* sail past the pier when his sister, Hanneke, cried that her kite was falling toward the witch's house. He turned to see it swoop to crash high upon the tiled roof. He ran to her and tried to work it free, but the string had caught itself fast; nothing he could do seemed able to free it.

A small crowd of other children soon gathered to watch his efforts. His friend, Gerrit, looked at him sympathetically and said, "It's no use, Jacob, you'll never get it down; it's lost."

Jacob almost agreed with him, but a glance at Hanneke's face stopped him. He surveyed the house and its roof. "I could climb up and get it."

Gerrit's jaw dropped. "Climb for it?" he gasped. "Climb the witch's house?"

Jacob frowned. "I don't believe she is really a witch. I don't believe in witches. She's just an old woman."

"A mean old woman," said Gerrit.

"An ugly old woman," another child said.

Jacob saw the other children nodding their heads.

"Nobody goes into her yard," a girl whispered, "let alone onto her roof."

For some reason her timidity made Jacob brave. "Well I shall," he boasted and, before he could loose his nerve, he strode to the gate of the small yard and went through it. Once inside he nearly turned back; it was a very small yard. What would he do if she came out? Where could he run? But he refused to give up.

He looked for a way to the roof. He saw that if he stood on the top of the fence he could jump to the casing on the top of a window. From there he believed he could reach the sill of a window on the second story. If he could scramble up to stand on it, it would be an easy jump to the roof over the door. From there, the rest of the roof would be easy to access.

So that is what he did. Reaching the sill of the second window was easy, as was pulling himself up to it, but getting his knees upon it proved very difficult; he could find nothing to grab hold to higher up. He nearly lost his grip several times, but grimly struggled on.

It would be far easier, if I didn't have to be so quiet.

But he finally succeeded. He took a moment to rest, and looked to his left at the roof over the door. It was a much longer jump than it had seemed from the ground. But he felt the eyes of all the children on him, and refused to admit defeat. He took a deep breath, backed to the right edge of the sill, ran, and jumped.

He made it with several feet to spare, but made quite a noise as he landed. He hugged the tiles and froze. Had the old witch heard him? He reminded himself that he did not believe in witches, but he was not as sure as he had been.

But she had apparently not heard for she did not appear, so he rose and carefully climbed to the peak and over to the kite. He quickly saw where the string had snagged, and freed it. He signaled Gerrit to take up the slack and, when he had, tossed the kite into the wind. It quickly rose and swept away, and Jacob began to descend.

But he then saw the ships.

The view was awesome from atop the roof. He could see far up and down the bay; he counted four, no, five ships in full sail. Without thinking, he sat and drank in the sight.

2

The best part of living in Amsterdam is this; watching the ships.

They came from all over the world. He loved to dream of their adventures and travels. He loved to watch their sails billow and snap in the breezes.

"Some day," he had told his father, "Some day, I shall sail on one of those ships to far off lands. I'll discover new lands; wonderful and exotic lands, that shall make me rich and famous."

His father had laughed and tousled his hair. "You were born a century too late, my liebkin," he had said, "I fear no lands are left for you to discover." He had turned back to his oven. "Those days of adventure and discovery are gone."

Jacob supposed his father was right; there were no lands left to discover. But he still lusted to see them.

Some day I shall.

He knew his mother expected him to remain and be a baker like his father, but his father had told him he did not expect he would and that he did not want him to.

"You must be the man you were meant to be," his father had said, "and you were not meant to be a baker."

Jacob liked his father.

"You there! What are you doing on my roof?"

Jacob jumped, lost his grip upon the tiles, and slid some feet before regaining it. The old hag herself was glaring up at him. She pointed her cane at him, and shook it threateningly. For a moment he feared she was hexing him.

"You get off my roof instantly."

But the scare she had given him had made him angry, and he shouted back, "Aw don't get your liver all aquiver. I'm not hurting anything."

She thumped her cane on the ground and shouted back, "My liver hasn't quivered in thirty years. And if my roof leaks the next time it rains, your father will be getting a bill. Get down."

The mention of his father sobered him, and he hurried to descend.

She met him on the ground and began to scold. But though she waved her cane about very liberally, she did not threaten to harm him.

He tried to appear properly chastened but a saucy grin escaped him. To his surprise it was answered by a grin from the old woman.

"Oh, get on with you, you little imp." She waved her cane at her gate, and he hurried to obey. But as he passed through it he heard her mutter, "Liver all aquiver," and cackle.

He ran to join Gerrit; he knew his friend had doubtless heard at least a part of their exchange and he couldn't wait to relate the remainder. But he then saw the boy was in serious conversation with a prosperous lady that Jacob recognized to be Mrs. DeGroot.

Jacob stopped in his tracks.

Mrs. DeGroot!

He glanced back at the old woman's house.

How much did she hear?

Does she know I was on the witch's house?

Mrs. DeGroot had very little patience for childish pranks and she was one of his father's best customers.

Will she tell my father on me?

But he heard Gerrit say, "There he is now, Mrs. DeGroot. I told you he would be back soon."

The lady turned and frowned at Jacob. "Jacob," she scolded, "where were you? You should not leave your sister unattended like this; she is only six."

"I'm only eight," Jacob wanted to retort. "That is only two years." But he didn't. Instead he pointed out as politely as he could that she was with Gerrit and that they were both with five other children she knew; some of whom were older than he.

"Nonetheless," she said severely. "She is your responsibility." Her face softened and she regarded him soberly for a moment. "Still Gerrit is a very responsible boy and a good friend of your family. Do you think your father would mind if you entrusted her to him while you ran a small errand for me?"

Jacob sighed. He was very relieved that she did not seem inclined to tell his father that he had left his sister alone; he did not want to have to explain to him why he had. Still, he did not want to 'run an errand' for her. But he forced himself to smile and reply, "I am sure he would not. What would you have me do?"

She removed a piece of paper from her purse and handed it to him.

"I am giving a party in two days and would like him to make the items on this list," she said. "I was on my way to him with it, but if you could run it to him, it would save me a good deal of time."

Jacob resisted the scowl that tried to escape him.

It will cost **me** *a good deal of time. Why can I not simply give the list to him when I go home?*

But he knew she would not accept that reasoning; children, to her, existed to do the bidding of their elders; their time had no value. So he again forced himself to smile and assured her he would be delighted to run the list to his father. Indeed a part of him was glad; he knew his father would be very happy to receive such a large order and would want to get as early a start on it as possible.

So, as soon as the pompous woman had thanked him and left, and he had ensured Gerrit did not mind tending his little sister, he set off running. But then he stopped.

While he had been on the witch's roof, besides watching the ships sail, he had noticed the alleys to his left led quite directly to Williamstrasse, the main road which led to his father's bakery.

There were only three turns. I'm sure there were.

He could picture them in his mind so clearly.

His father had often warned him to remain on the main roads. "It is far too easy to get lost in the alleys," he had said.

But how can I get lost if there are only three turns and I know right where they are? And it will save me at least ten minutes.

He determined he would take the alleys and began his run again. When he reached the first alley he hesitated; he did not like disobeying his father, but then made the turn.

If I wasn't afraid to climb the witch's roof, why should I be afraid to run through a few alleys?

Everything went fine as he quickly came to the first turn he had remembered. He zoomed around it and picked up his pace. It bothered him a little that the second alley curved to the left; he hadn't remembered it doing so, but he quickly came to next turn and was relieved to see it looked just like it should.

One more alley and I'll be at Williamstasse.

He felt rather proud of himself. But when he made the final turn he stopped in dismay. It was obvious this alley did not lead to Williamstrasse; it went only a very short distance and then branched into two.

I'm sure there were no branches on any of the alleys I saw from the roof.

He turned back to the alley he had just left.

I'll have to backtrack.

He felt sure he could.

But he then saw that this alley also very quickly branched into two.

I didn't notice another alley joining it.

Which branch was the one he had come by?

His heart sank as he realized he didn't know.

Why, oh, why did I not stay on the main roads as father ordered?

He had just decided to try the right branch when two men stepped from a pub and came toward him. He didn't know them, and considered running, but one called, "Hold on there, boy. We mean you no harm." Jacob stared back at them, and saw they did indeed appear friendly.

"You just look like you could use some help," said the shorter of the two with a wink. "Are you lost?"

Jacob considered the question; should he trust them? It was too late to run; the men were already by his side. "Can you tell me how to get to Williamstrasse?" he finally asked.

"Well now . . ." The short man pursed his lips, and ran his hand through his hair. "I could tell you, but it's a bit complicated." He turned to his companion. "Four, or maybe five turns isn't it?"

The other man nodded soberly, and Jacob's heart fell.

"Ah, but it so happens," said the short man cheerfully, "that my friend and I happen to be going nigh there ourselves." "He reached out, and clapped Jacob on the shoulder amiably. "Follow us, lad, and we'll lead you there straightaway."

Jacob grinned up at him and agreed. He decided he liked these men. They led him to the left, and he followed them.

Father shall never know. I'll be back on the main roads soon, and then I'll run to make up for the time I lost.

The men led him quite a ways; Jacob began to get tired.

I may as well have stayed on the main road; this isn't any shorter at all.

There was a whiff of cold salty air. They were very near the water.

This is wrong. Williamstrasse is not near the water.

"I think we are lost," he said. "There is the bay."

The little man laughed, and said, "Oh, we're not lost."

The way he emphasized the word 'we' made Jacob stare at him alarmed.

The men were considering him with sly grins.

Jacob turned to run.

"Ah, no you don't," the short man said as he grabbed Jacob by the arm.

Jacob struggled and kicked, but he received an awful blow to the back of his head, and everything went black.

2 Shanghaied

May, 1763

When Jacob awoke he was lying on rough sawn uneven boards. He could see nothing.

W . . Why can I not see? W . . Where am I?

He lay frozen. He could not see, but heard . . . far-off boots and harsh voices, creaks and groans of timber such as he had only before heard in a violent wind storm but without the sound of wind, and underneath it all, a very quiet shush, shush, shush.

Wherever he was it stank, but most of the odors seemed unfamiliar except . . . salt, mold, unwashed bodies, and . . . urine. He realized the last was coming from him; he had wet himself.

The warm wetness spread and pooled beneath him. He sat up and immediately regretted it for he hit his head which was already throbbing with pain. The pain made him woozy; he had to struggle not to vomit, but refused to yield to the impulse. It was bad enough to sit in a pool of urine; he would not loose control of his stomach.

He carefully felt the shelf above himself; it was only about a yard from the floor. He felt to his left, and found the wall. He followed it all around himself, and found he was confined in a tiny room about six feet long by four feet wide. But it was narrower at one end, and one wall was not perpendicular; it tapered out several inches. The opposite wall contained a door, firmly locked.

Where am I?

His disorientation was growing worse; the entire room seemed to be moving, rocking. The vomit came; he was covered in it. The smell rose and mingled with the myriad other odors, and his stomach retched again and again. It was horrid, and the room was too small to get away from it.

He heard footsteps outside the door, and kicked at it yelling, "Help me! Please, let me out."

The door was thrown open, and he was blinded by the light. Even in his terror, Jacob was relieved; he could see! He shielded his eyes, and saw the light came from a lantern held by the largest man he had ever seen.

Jacob's instinct was to flee, but to where? He could see nothing beyond the man, and he could not get past him anyway. He hid his face, and cowered.

"Here now, shut your mouth." The hulk of a man spoke with a harsh voice and was missing numerous teeth, but his tone was not unkind. His visage contorted into a horrible smile. "You don't want to let Jamie hear you going on like that, or the captain either. They wouldn't like it, see?"

His great nose wrinkled, and he waved a ham sized hand before it. "You made a proper mess of yourself, didn't you?" He didn't wait for an answer, but turned away saying, "Ah well, likely you couldn't help it." He glanced over his shoulder at Jacob. "It's your first time to sea, I'd 'spec."

To sea? We're at sea?

Jacob stared mutely, both terrified and excited, but the man reached back and effortlessly hauled him from the room which Jacob then saw was nothing more than a closet built into the wall roughly a yard above the floor.

"Come on with you," the hulk grunted, and Jacob followed him to a ladder that led to a small hatch in the ceiling.

"You stay there."

Jacob watched as the man climbed the ladder with surprising ease. For such a massive man he was very agile.

Jacob stared around himself. His eyes had adjusted to the light, and he now found the lantern very dim indeed, but he could see he was in a long hall with many rude shelves. At one end was the door to the closet in which he had found himself, and the other was obscured in the darkness.

This is what the inside of a ship looks like? I'm inside a real ship? Wait until Gerrit hears I was inside a ship!

He suddenly found a bucket being lowered from the hatch above him.

"Well, don't stand there staring at it," he was ordered. "Unhook it."

Jacob saw it was suspended from a hook on the end of a rope. He lifted it off with some difficulty, and quickly set it down; it was very heavy. It was quickly followed by a second bucket, and then a third. It was all Jacob could do to lift down the second bucket, and he watched the third come down with dismay, but the man ordered him to step aside, and it was lowered to the floor, and the rope allowed to dangle.

"Not very stout, are you?" asked the man as he slid down the ladder.

Jacob bristled. "I'm only eight. What do you expect?"

The hulk grunted, and said, "I expect you'll learn to work more hearty, or wish you had. There're those less patient than I." He crossed his arms. "Strip off your clothes."

"What?"

"Are you deaf? Strip off your clothes." The thick eyebrows went down. "Step lively now."

Jacob was afraid and stripped quickly. He had hardly removed the last article when he was inundated by a cold bucket of water dumped over his head. It was salty, and made the back of his head burn like fire. He put his hand to his head, and found it was caked with blood. He stood naked and dazed, and watched the water find its way to cracks in the floor and disappear.

The man was already climbing the ladder. "Clean your clothes in one of the other buckets, and then use them both to flush out the mess you made. I'll leave you the lantern; see you don't make a fire with it."

Jacob stared up at him. Despite his brutishness, he was company. Jacob did not wish to be left alone. "Please, sir," he called. "What is your name?"

"Eh?" The hulk gazed back at him for a moment before saying, "You can call me Isaac."

"Isaac! Are you a Jew?"

Isaac dropped with a thud, and backhanded him, throwing him against the shelves. He then picked him up, and held him dangling inches from his face. "I aint no filthy Jew!"

"I'm a Jew," Jacob managed to whisper.

The huge man scowled at him for a moment, and then set him on his feet. "I wouldn't make that common knowledge were I you." He again climbed the ladder.

He glanced down from the hatch, and said, "I'll be back with some food and water by and by. See you do a good job cleaning up." The hatch was slammed shut.

Jacob stared at the buckets. *Why should I have to work for him? Who is he to tell me what to do? He's not my father.*

His father! The cold reality engulfed him and he sank to his knees. His father did not know where he was. His father could not help him.

A cold panic rose from deep within him and threatened to choke him. He wanted to go home. He had to get off this ship! He stared at the hatch Isaac had left by. Did he dare follow him?

Very quietly, he crept up the ladder, and pushed at the hatch. It would not open! Franticly he searched for a handle or latch, but could find nothing.

He was locked in.

He carefully descended again. He mustn't make a sound. He took the lantern, and crept down the aisle between the shelves, but it ended with a bare wall. He held the lantern up, and stared into one of the shelves, but it was so deep he could not see to its end; only darkness.

The void was frightening, and he shuddered and ran back to under the hatch.

He sat down beside his clothes. He could not escape. He might never see his father again, or his mother . . . his sisters. He pushed at the knowledge tentatively like a loose tooth. It hurt.

"God," he cried silently. "God of Abraham, Isaac . . ." He paused. *Isaac?* "The real Isaac," he prayed, "and Jacob . . . the real Jacob." The duplicity of the names was confusing him. He couldn't think; his head hurt. He knew God knew which Jacob he meant. "God," he wept, "help me."

He didn't know how long he sat crying before he again stood and noticed the buckets. He remembered Isaac's orders to clean his clothes and the closet. He didn't want to clean them.

But he thought he should at least clean his clothes; he was sure he would not get any others, he could not continue naked, and he did not want to don them as they were. So he did his best to cleanse them in one of the buckets. He then laid them out on one of the shelves to dry.

But he determined he would not . . . would not! . . . cleanse the closet. He sat down against the shelves defiantly.

But he then heard footsteps come to the hatch, and an image of what Isaac might do to him if he found the room untouched sprang to his mind, and he jumped up. Luckily the steps continued past. Reluctantly he dragged the third bucket to the door of the room.

But how am I to cleanse it, he wondered. He had no rags or mop to do so. He remembered how Isaac had dumped the first bucket over his head and allowed the water to run out the cracks in the floor. He carefully hefted the heavy bucket over his head, and dashed the water at the mess of vomit. He leaped out of the way as the water sloshed back at him.

Most of the filth disappeared through the cracks, but some remained. He dumped the bucket he had used for his clothes. The closet floor was now almost clean, but a puddle of filth was trapped in a corner. How was he to get it out? He realized he would have to wipe it out with his hands. He had to struggle to prevent retching, but he succeeded in getting the corner reasonably clean. He decided it would have to do.

The closet was clean, but his hands were not. How was he to cleanse them? He had nothing to wipe them on. There were his clothes, but if he wiped his hands on them, they would again be filthy. He finally decided he could spare his underwear. He wiped his hands as clean as he could, threw his underwear into the depths of a shelf, and donned his remaining clothes. They were not yet dry, but he was tired of being naked.

He found a dry part of the floor and sat down to await Isaac's return.

What is to become of me?

He struggled against the urge to again cry.

The lantern sputtered and went out. He was left in darkness.

He struggled to fight the terror that threatened to overwhelm him. He forced himself to concentrate upon the sounds and smells surrounding him.

This is one of those ships I have always fantasized about. I'm on a ship! Will it take me to far away lands?

But it was no good. This was not at all as he had imagined! He just wanted to go home. Would he ever see his home again? He tried to hold to the memory of his father's face; would he ever see him again? Or Hannecke? Gerrit? His mother? He tried to remember his mother's
face, but for some reason he couldn't quite do so, and the harder he tried, the more indistinct it became.

He buried his head in his arms and wept.

3   The Sea

June, 1763

Jacob soon learned his new life consisted of very long periods of inactivity and isolation broken by frenetic hard labor surrounded by brutal men. The darkness would be broken by the hatch being thrown open; men would drop down, and he would be thrust onto a shelf with a wiry little demon named Arturo. Arturo would crawl to the back of the shelves which Jacob had discovered were very deep. It would then be Jacob's task to drag whatever boxes or bundles the other men threw onto the shelf back to Arturo who would pack them securely away.

No matter how fast Jacob worked, he could never satisfy the little man and a steady stream of curses, kicks, and beatings would rain down upon him. Then suddenly the flow of packages would cease, the other men would disappear, Jacob would quickly pull the remainder to Arturo and, with a final curse, the dwarf himself would crawl from the shelf and climb the ladder. The hatch would be slammed shut, and Jacob left in the darkness to nurse his new bruises.

But as terrible as was the labor, Jacob preferred it to the horrifying black solitude when the hatch would be opened only to allow someone to exchange a bowl of whatever it was they fed him for the bucket in which he relieved himself. He had never decided what it was in the bowl, but had learned to bolt the greasy mess immediately for as soon as his bucket was returned empty, the bowl was demanded. The mess served as both his food and water; he longed for a drink of fresh water. As the shelves were filled, the air grew increasingly stifling.

At last the shelves could hold no more and first his closet and then the aisle was packed until he was left in a tiny den at the base of the ladder and then even that was filled until he was unable to stand, and lay under the hatch in a space even more confining than the closet he had awakened in. The hatch sealed even the tiniest breath of air and the heat was nearly unbearable.

Finally the hatch was opened, and Isaac reached down, plucked him out, and threw him to the deck. Jacob lay for a moment in the blindingly bright sun drinking in the gloriously cool salty breeze. Towering over him were sails filled with power. He sprang to his feet, and looked to his massive friend.

Jacob considered Isaac to be his friend, for he alone of the men had made the effort to explain what was expected of him without cuffs and curses and on several occasions had come to his aid when the cuffs had become too liberal.

"What must I do?" he asked.

The man shrugged, and smiled. "Whatever you've a mind to. The captain said you need exercise and sun." He raised an eyebrow. "Just mind you avoid certain men." He grinned. "I think you know which ones I mean."

Jacob did know. Most of the men had little tolerance if he annoyed them but some seemed to take pleasure in abusing him regardless of his actions. A few others seemed to like him, but something about their behavior always made him uncomfortable; he did not want to be alone with them.

The deck was rolling beneath him, but he hardly noticed it as he raced to the rail to stare delightedly at the endless blue expanse of the sea. For years he had fantasized of this very vista, traveling to unknown lands.

The thought of all that water between him and his family was distressing, but oh, it was beautiful and filled him with excitement. The burly Isaac came to lean upon the rail beside him, and Jacob grinned up at him.

"It sure is a glory isn't it?" Isaac said. "A man'd do most anything he had to do for this." He glared down upon Jacob; Jacob shrank away from him. The man turned his back, and began to walk away but not before snarling, "Mind you stay out of my way too."

Jacob stood and watched him go. The sun seemed to have lost its brightness, the sea its delight. What had he done to cause this anger and rejection? He did not know.

The remainder of the voyage he was left at his liberty. He was given much better food and allowed a ration of water. He was careful to avoid certain men, but with others became quite friendly. They seemed to enjoy his antics and occasionally gave him some rum which made him quite giddy and silly; the men would roar with laughter.

The captain himself issued orders Jacob was not to be struck under any condition and Jacob's bruises began to fade. Despite his homesickness, he began to enjoy himself.

But Isaac took care to avoid him, and this distressed Jacob. Of all the men, Isaac was the one he most liked. But Isaac no longer seemed to like him.

Finally one day land was sighted. Jacob was allowed to climb the ropes to the bird's nest and shown the shadowy mass rising along the horizon. The lookout clapped him on the back. "That is America, lad. We'll be docked soon in Philadelphia. You ever hear of Philadelphia?"

Jacob shook his head.

"Well soon enough you'll see it with your own eyes."

Jacob stared at him. He did not know why, but the man's voice had suddenly turned cold. The lookout indicated the rope. "Get down with you."

Jacob climbed down. What had he done?

16

The captain himself was awaiting him. "Jacob," he said, "we'll be in Philadelphia on the morrow. I'll need you to accompany me into the city; see you're ready." He looked him over and sniffed. "Clean yourself up; take a bath and wash your clothes." He turned on his heel and left.

Jacob found a bucket, tied it to a rope, and hoisted water from the sea to do as he had been ordered, but he found Isaac beside him. The man would not look at him, but asked quietly, "Can you swim, boy?"

Jacob shook his head. *Why is he talking to me now? He sounds almost friendly.* He didn't care why; he was just glad he was. He realized Isaac was not looking at him and so had not seen him shake his head. He whispered, "No."

The man sighed. "Too bad. You could easily have escaped by swimming to shore as we slipped up the river." He glanced at Jacob, and then away.

"Listen to me boy. Soon as we dock, you get yourself on shore any way you can, and run." He glared at him a second. "You hear me? Run; as far and as fast as you can." He turned and lumbered quickly away.

4 Sold

August, 1763

Jacob stood on the wharf staring at Philadelphia. He was in a foreign land as he had always dreamed. It was terrifying and exhilarating at the same time. What would he find when the captain took him into the city?

He remembered Isaac's warning for him to run at his earliest opportunity. If he was going to run this was his chance. The captain had led him from the ship, but had then gone to give instructions to the men already busily unloading the cargo. He had left Jacob with the wharfinger, the owner of the wharf, with strict orders not to wander.

Jacob glanced at the wharfinger. He was a fat old man who was intently making entries into a large ledger.

I could just walk away, and he would likely not even notice. And if he did, I could easily outrun him. He glanced to where the captain was berating his crew. They were so far away they could not catch him either even if they saw him, which they probably would not. *If I am going to run, I should go now.*

But where could he run to? He peered at the city spread before him. He knew nothing about Philadelphia. The thought of being lost in a foreign city was terrifying.

And if the captain did catch him, what would he do? He shuddered to think of the beating he would receive. And he would almost certainly be returned to the dark hold. He had the run of the ship; presumably because he had always obeyed his orders. Everyone was friendly to him; well, almost everyone. Why should he risk losing all of that?

Because Isaac had told him to. Despite how Isaac had treated him for most of the voyage, Jacob still considered him his friend. He trusted him; Isaac had never lied to him. If Isaac had told him to run, he must have had a reason.

But why should he run when the risk was so great? How would he live, where would he go? He gazed again at the city. The warehouses of the wharf blocked his view of much of the city, but he could see the road which he would have to take. Or should he instead only hide in one of the warehouses?

He looked over the warehouse before him. Could they find him in there? He could hide and then decide what to do.

Or should he run down the road?

Then he heard the captain calling him. He looked up to see he had returned and was beckoning him to come. His opportunity to run had passed. With a mixture of despair and relief he went to him.

The captain led him into the city. Jacob was soon entranced with the novel sights and sounds. The people spoke a strange language which he could not understand. He ventured to ask the captain what language it was. The captain was not one you asked trivial questions of; he tolerated little aggravation, but he answered shortly, "English".

English. So Philadelphia is an English colony. Jacob knew they were not in England.

After a long walk, the captain led him into a tavern. Jacob had never been into a tavern before, but he knew it was a tavern even before they had entered it. Clearly taverns in Philadelphia were much the same as those in Amsterdam.

The captain sat at a table, and ordered a tall stein of beer. He spoke English. He did not invite Jacob to sit, so Jacob stood and waited while the captain slowly savored his beer. Jacob was very thirsty, and wished the captain would give him something to drink, but he did not.

Soon the captain finished, and hove himself from the bench, and they left the tavern. Jacob gazed at the sign over the door as they left; Indian King. He could not understand the words but he sounded them out to himself; In-die-un K-eeng. He liked the sound of the words; they were exotic. He wondered what they meant.

"Jacob," he heard the captain bark.

He realized he had dawdled. The captain was scowling back at him. He hurried to catch up. They soon entered a large open market. Jacob reveled in the strange and wonderful smells, and his stomach rumbled with hunger. But the crowds of people made him nervous, and he made sure to stay close to the captain who strode quickly straight along the road with nary a glance to the left or right.

But then the captain stopped so suddenly Jacob ran into him. "Ha," the captain said happily. "This is fortuitous." He grinned down upon Jacob. "We happened to come on a sale day. This shall save me a great deal of time."

He hurried over to a man sitting at a desk with a large ledger before him. Jacob followed him. The captain produced a paper from his pocket, and addressed the man. He spoke rapidly in English, and gestured several times at Jacob.

Jacob wished he knew what he was saying. It made him anxious to be talked about like that.

The man studied the paper, and considered Jacob carefully. Jacob grew more fearful. He looked around. *Perhaps I should flee. I could easily lose myself in the crowd.*

But the captain's hand clapped hold of him. Jacob stared up to see him glaring at him. "Don't you even think of running,

Jacob." He lowered his face to within inches of Jacob's. "Don't –
you – dare."

Jacob did not dare. He stood and watched as the man
wrote his name in the ledger. Next to his name the man wrote 21.
*What does that mean? Why did the captain bring me here? Why
did he have the man write my name in his ledger?* He glanced at
the captain, but said nothing.

Very soon a large number of men, women, and children
filed into the yard and were herded into a group at one side. Jacob
noticed everyone inspected these people closely. What was
happening?

"Jacob," said the captain, "go and join those people."
When Jacob hesitated, his eyebrows went down, and he barked,
"Go."

Jacob went.

When he looked back, the captain was standing scowling at
him. He shrank into himself. *Why is he angry with me? What
are they going to do to me?*

People began to be taken from the group and led into the
center of the crowd. Jacob could not see what was happening, but
he heard one man who talked very fast who was interrupted often
by individuals who would call out one or two words. Then the fast
talking man would continue. Finally there would be the bang of a
hammer on a desk, and they would come for another one of the
group.

Jacob was terrified to notice that the people taken never
returned.

Then they came for him. He searched desperately for the
captain, but he could not see him.

He was led to a box and made to stand upon it. Four or
five men came and felt him all over; even made him open his
mouth so they could look within it. *How do they dare treat me
so?* But they did dare, and no one stopped them. There was
nothing he could do to stop them either.

Finally they stopped and the fast talking man began to talk.
Again there were the interruptions. Finally the fast talker took a
gavel and banged it upon his desk.

A large man came and, seizing his arm, tried to lead Jacob away. Jacob did not like the large man and fought to escape. But the man simply picked him up, carried him bodily through the crowd, and threw him to the ground. He then scowled down upon him and spoke harshly.

Jacob was terrified. "I don't understand you," he pled. "I don't know what you want me to do."

The man frowned, and then looked about himself and called out something. Jacob heard the word, 'Dutch'. The man called again, and finally a man came. The large man said some more things, and the other man replied. After a bit the large man walked over to a bench and sat while the other man addressed himself to Jacob.

"Your new master asked me to talk to you."

"My . . . my master!" Jacob cried. "How could he be my master? Am I now a slave?"

"Wouldn't spit for the difference," the man said. He regarded Jacob. "Do you mean you don't know? No, I can see you do not." He shook his head. "I expect your father did not tell you."

"Did not tell me what?"

"That he sold your labor to pay for your voyage to the Americas."

Jacob stared at him. *Could it be true? Did my father really sell me?* No! He did not believe it.

The Dutchman considered him pitying. "Did you think your captain had agreed to transport you across the sea for nothing?"

But . . . but, the captain took me across the sea against my father's will. My father did not ask him to. His heart quaked. *He didn't, did he? No. Of course he did not!*

The Dutchman put his hand upon his shoulder. "I'm sure your father meant to explain it to you before you arrived in Philadelphia."

"My father is not here," Jacob said.

"I know," said the Dutchman soberly. "Nor your mother either. The captain told the magistrate."

Jacob was surprised. *The captain told the magistrate that I had been kidnapped?* Then why had they sold him to pay for his voyage?

"It is a shame they both died on the crossing," said the Dutchman. "Ah, but those things happen."

"What?" cried Jacob. "But . . . but"

The Dutchman wasn't listening. "Had they lived it would not be so bad for you. You'd have been with them, and in seven years you'd have all been free to do as you chose." He regarded Jacob sadly. "But now, poor lad, you're all alone, and you've got to pay for the passage of all three of you." He shook his head. "Twenty one years! You may as well be a slave."

"But my parents did not die," Jacob finally managed to cry. "It is a lie!" In a torrent of words he poured out the whole tale of his kidnapping. "You must tell the magistrate. I should not have been sold. The captain lied."

The Dutchman squatted upon his heels and ran his hand through his hair. "The captain had a paper your father had signed. The magistrate certified it."

"But the captain lied. My father never signed that paper."

The Dutchman shook his head. "It is too late. Your services have been legally sold. They belong to your master now."

"But," Jacob looked around frantically. What could he do? He stared back at the Dutchman pleadingly. "They should not have been sold! Please . . ."

The Dutchman stared at the ground, and Jacob's heart sank. The man wasn't going to help him. Was there anyone else who could speak Dutch? None that he knew.

He dropped to his knees at the Dutchman's feet and stared up into his face.

"Help me," he whispered.

"I'll give you a word of advice, boy," the man said quietly but firmly. "Don't waste your time fretting about what should be. What should be is usually not what is. And the only thing anyone cares about is what is.

"Maybe it's right you should have to labor for your master and maybe it is not." He leaned close to Jacob's face.

"Irregardless, you do have to labor for him. He bought your labor for the next twenty one years and you can bet your last shilling the law'll make sure he gets every day of those twenty one years."

He stood back. "That's what is. The sooner you accept it the better off you'll be." He pointed at the loathsome man. "Get yourself over there and follow him home. See you do whatever he orders you to do and you'll be all right."

Jacob started to obey but then turned back fearfully. "I can't understand him. How can I know what he wants from me?"

"I expect you'll learn. Now go!" The Dutchman turned away, and Jacob slowly walked to the large man.

His master said something and turned to stride away. Jacob assumed he was to follow him, so he did. They walked out of the city and several miles to the southwest. They came to a small village named Wynnewood and turned into a small courtyard formed by a house on the left, a barn on the right, and a mill on the far side. Beyond the mill was the small river his master called Karakung. The fourth side of the courtyard was formed by the fence through which they had entered.

Jacob was impressed. Everything was clean and well built; his new master was clearly prosperous.

He was not led to the house but to the barn. His master pointed at an empty stall next to one occupied by a pair of old horses. Jacob walked into it and his master shut the door on him, turned on his heel, and went into the house.

What am I to do now? He considered trying to run, but he remembered the Dutchman had told him the law would make sure he served his master. Besides, the door was latched on the outside. He sat on the straw and waited to see what would happen.

By and by the master returned, opened the door, and put a bowl of stew in the corner of the stall. It smelled good and Jacob was very hungry so he went over to get it.

But before he reached it, his master grabbed him and flung him out of the stall onto the floor of the barn.

Jacob lay cowering. *What have I done wrong? Didn't he mean for me to eat the stew? Why then did he bring it?*

His master lumbered to him and kicked him savagely several times and then dropped to his knees to methodically rain blows upon him.

Jacob covered his face and writhed upon the floor trying to convey suitable contrition for whatever his offense had been, but the blows continued. Dimly he realized his master was laughing!

Quite abruptly the man stopped his beating, groaned to his feet, dragged Jacob to his stall, and threw him in. The door was slammed shut, the latch was thrown, and the beast lumbered from the barn.

The bowl of food was still there, but Jacob was afraid to touch it for a long time. Finally his hunger overcame his fear and he crept over to it. It hurt to move. The stew was cold and had many flies buzzing about it but it still tasted good and he ate it thankfully.

He lay down and tried to sleep. He remembered Isaac's warning to flee as soon as the ship had docked. Why, oh why had he not obeyed?

The next morning he was awakened by another beating. Again his new master laughed. He had brought a fat ugly girl with him that he called Miranda. She sat and watched his master beat him and laughed with him.

When the beating was over, his master pointed at Miranda and said some things emphatically. Jacob did not understand most of it but did manage to surmise she was his master's daughter and that he was to obey her also. Fortunately many words of English were similar to Dutch words; including 'daughter'.

Maybe learning English shall not be so hard after all. But he hurt far too much to feel glad of that discovery.

5   The Sablonskis

October, 1763

Seated upon the mare, Molly, in the stall she shared with Bobby, the gelding, Jacob pretended he was a knight of old and the evil Sir Thomas was challenging him to a joust. It was a foolish game and not much fun, but it helped to pass the time and the horses seemed to enjoy his company and tolerate his oddness.

The game was interrupted by his master's harsh call. Jacob was almost glad; he welcomed a day when he was given more work than the morning and evening chores. Work was preferable to the weary hours of leisure. Had he been allowed to leave the barn they would have been far easier to fill, but this was forbidden. He must be instantly available when called for.

When he presented himself to his master, he found him accompanied by a tall blond man and a ten or eleven year old boy with the reddest hair Jacob had ever seen. The man smiled at him and said in very poor Dutch, "Your master has loaned you to us for the day. We are going to . . ." The man paused, and then turned to the boy to ask in German, "What is the Dutch word for 'harvest'?"

"You speak German?" Jacob cried.

The man and boy stared at him. "Do you?"

"Yes," Jacob said. "My parents were German; well, Austrian really. We spoke German at home."

The man clapped him on the shoulder. "Well then, that solves that problem. We are going to harvest our corn field today. Dick here . . ." He indicated his son. "Saw that the miller had a new indentured boy and suggested we ask to rent him. Your master was kind enough to loan you to us. I hope you do not mind."

Jacob was shocked, and glanced at the boy. *Is that his nickname? His father seems so nice, yet he humiliates him so?* 'Dick,' in German, was 'thick' or 'fat'. Yet he noticed the boy did not seem offended.

"Come." The man led Jacob and his son to a buckboard who's right side was exceedingly tall. But Jacob had no time to marvel at the oddity before he and the boy had scrambled into the back and the father was driving them away. Jacob saw the side was really several planks which had been attached together and joined to the real side which was the same height as the left.

The boy took his hand and shook it. "My name is Dick," he said. "Well really Richard, but everyone calls me Dick. What is your name?"

"My name is Jacob." He leaned close to Dick and quietly asked, "Why do they call you 'Dick'? You are not fat."

The boy burst out laughing and then, to Jacob's dismay, told his father what Jacob had said, and his father also laughed.

"Dick doesn't mean fat," the boy said. He grinned. "Well, it does, but not when it's a name. Dick is just what people call a boy who's real name is Richard."

"Why?" 'Dick' sounded nothing like 'Richard'.

Dick shrugged and laughed. "I don't know; they just do."

Miranda walked past them and Dick leaned to Jacob's ear and whispered, "Now she should be called 'dick'!"

Jacob laughed so hard he got a stitch in his side. He couldn't stop laughing though because every time he did, Dick would giggle and they would start again.

The joke was not really that funny, Jacob thought, but it felt good to be with another boy, especially one as nice as Dick.

Jacob was surprised they were driving as far as they were; they had gone nearly a mile, he guessed. "You came all this way to fetch me?"

"What?" asked Dick. Understanding dawned on his face. "Oh, no. We don't live on our farm. We live right next to you; to the mill."

"Why don't you live on your farm?"

"No one does," answered Dick. "Well, almost no one. Everyone lives in the village."

"Why?"

"Well, because of the Injins, I guess. It's safer."

"Indians?" cried Jacob. He had hoped he would meet an Indian. "There are Indians around here?"

"No. Not around here. There hasn't been any Injins around these parts for . . . I don't know. A long time."

"Why do you call them Injins?" asked Jacob. "I thought they were called Indians."

"Well, they are supposed to be," Dick agreed. He shrugged and grinned. "But everyone calls them 'Injins'."

Jacob frowned. *Americans are hard people to understand. They call boys who are named Richard, 'Dick', and they call Indians, 'Injins.'* But then he grinned back at Dick. He didn't care if he couldn't understand them; he liked them.

When they got to the field Jacob stood and stared. He realized Dick and his father were watching him amused and blushed but he couldn't help it. It was the first time he had ever seen a corn plant although he had seen corn ears. He had always wondered why they were called ears. Now he understood; growing half way down a tall stalk, they did resemble ears.

Dick's father showed him how to shuck off the leaves surrounding an ear and break it free before throwing it into the buckboard.

"We'll have you pluck the corn from the first row while Dick takes the second row and half of the third and I'll take the other half of the third and all of the fourth and fifth rows."

Jacob saw that the high side of the wagon kept the corn from flying past the buckboard; in fact, Dick and his father threw the corn to hit the side. He watched in wonder as ears from their rows seemed to fly in an unending stream over his head. "You are really fast."

"We're not so fast," the father said. "A good shucker can keep two ears in the air all the time."

"Wow," Jacob gasped, but Dick only groaned.

"Don't listen to him, Jacob. It's an old joke and not that good of one." Turning to his father he demanded, "Go on. Tell him the punch line."

His father laughed. "He keeps the ears on the side of his head in the air."

Dick rolled his eyes. "Didn't I warn you?" he muttered, but Jacob laughed and hurried to keep up with them.

We'll soon be past the buckboard. Should I lead the horse forward? But he didn't have to; the horse moved forward by himself. Jacob stood and gaped, but Dick and his father laughed at him.

"Barney's been doing this longer than I have." Dick said. "He doesn't need anyone to tell him what to do."

Jacob's hands hurt; they were raw with dozens of tiny cuts from the corn leaves. He tried to hide his discomfort; working in the fresh cool air with jolly companions who seemed to like him was far too pleasant; he wanted nothing to ruin it. But Dick's father appeared by his side and, grabbing one of his hands, inspected it.

"They're not used to such work yet," he said. "It's too bad." He released the hand and shook his head. "I wish I could help you, but the only way to toughen them up is to work with them. If it gets too bad, I have a salve in the front of the buckboard you can use to cut the sting."

Jacob shook his head. If Dick and his father could stand it, then so could he. He went back to shucking, and Dick's father patted him on the back and began back to his own rows.

"Excuse me, sir," Jacob called after him. "What should I call you?"

29

The man returned. "I'm sorry. I forgot I had not introduced myself." He held out his hand. "I am Mr. Sablonski."

Jacob shook his hand. "I am very pleased to meet you."

"And I you." Mr. Sablonski ruffled Jacob's hair and grinned. "Very pleased indeed."

They worked hard until midday, and then stopped to eat from a bag the father produced from under the buckboard seat. It was only bread and cheese, but there was plenty and it was shared generously with Jacob. He thought he had never eaten anything so good.

When the meal was over, Jacob got up, and realized he was stiff and sore. He almost wished they had not stopped to eat.

He turned wearily back to the corn, but Mr. Sablonski said, "It's not good for a boy to work just after he's eaten. Dick, why don't you take Jake for a good long walk through the woods?"

Jacob's jaw dropped. He had never heard of a father who would send his son off to play when there was work to be done. Even his own father had never done such a thing. And Dick's father had called him 'Jake' instead of Jacob. He decided he liked it.

He followed Dick into the forest surrounding the fields. He had never been in a forest before, although when he told Dick, Dick laughed and assured him it was not a forest. It was only a wood lot, and not a very big one at that. Jacob could only stare at him in amazement. It looked like a forest to him. Nearly an hour slipped by.

When they returned to the field Jacob saw Mr. Sablonski had done five rows by himself. He felt ashamed and determined he would work extra hard the rest of the afternoon to make up for it. But he noticed he wasn't at all stiff or sore. Maybe Dick's father had been right about taking a break.

By the middle of the afternoon there was only one row to be done. "I'll finish it myself," Mr. Sablonski said to Dick. "Why don't you take Jake and see how the apples are doing?"

"Come on," Dick said, and took off running to the corner of the wood lot where several apple trees stood. Jacob ran to catch up.

But when he caught him, Dick ran faster. The two boys raced to the trees and threw themselves to the ground panting. Dick had won, but not by much. Jacob could not remember when he had had so much fun.

The apples were still a little hard, but Dick picked eight anyway and they walked back to the buckboard eating them. The last row had been done, they climbed into the back upon the corn, and Dick's father began the drive home. They gave him two of the apples and he thanked them.

Jacob was sitting watching the trees go by when he felt a seed hit him on the cheek. Dick had spit it at him. Fortunately he had a core of his own, and quickly returned the favor. They were soon engaged in a full fledged war until Mr. Sablonski yelled at them to stop.

"What do you think you're doing to that corn, jumping about on it as you are?"

They stopped, but Jacob could see he was not really angry at them.

All too soon they turned into the mill courtyard. Jacob saw his master was standing talking with a large boisterous man. Dick scowled at the man. "That's Mr. O'Connel," he said.

"You don't like him," Jacob observed.

Dick sniffed. "Neither shall you. You'll see."

Jacob scrambled from the buckboard, and watched Dick and his father drive away. He hoped they would 'borrow' him again some day soon. *Why could they not have bought me instead of . . .* He glanced at his master. *Instead of him.*

Mr. O'Connel said something with a sneer. Jacob looked at the man and saw he was staring at him. He said something else to the miller.

Jacob realized the stranger was making fun of him; more than that, was making fun of his master. He crossed his arms, and glared at the man. *Who is this arrogant man to come into my master's mill and taunt him?*

He looked at his master, but was dismayed to see he was making no effort to defend himself. He was acting like a whipped pup which had made a mess on the floor.

What is the matter with him? Jacob found himself despising him.

His master pointed to the barn, and Jacob went.

It was not long before he heard Mr. O'Connel leave.

Soon after, the miller came and beat Jacob. He hadn't beaten him in almost a week.

Jacob could not understand. *Did he not tell me to go with Dick and his father? Why does he never tell me what I've done wrong?*

6 Submission

December, 1763

Jacob walked wearily down the road toward the mill. He had been working since long before dawn and the sun was very low but he had finished moving the stone fence, all four hundred feet of it, ten feet to the west. He was eager to lie down; his muscles were throbbing.

He heard Mr. Sablonski's wagon before it came around the bend, and stepped off the road to wait for it. It was easy to hear and recognize his wagon because of the noise of the tin pans and tubs. No matter how carefully they were packed, they still clattered.

The tinker came around the bend and pulled up beside him with a smile.

"Hey there, Jake the snake," he called. "You want a ride back to the mill?"

Jacob grinned, and hurried to climb up beside the tinker. Mr. Sablonski always called him 'Jake the snake'; he said Jacob with his quiet graceful movements reminded him of a snake; besides, 'Jake' rhymed with 'snake'. It felt good to have a nickname, especially one that made him sound dangerous.

The man clicked to his horse, and they began rolling.

Jacob asked, "You coming back from another trip?" Mr. Sablonski made regular trips far into the surrounding countryside selling his wares and making repairs. Jacob envied him. He wished he could travel far and wide and meet all kinds of people.

"Yep," the tinker said. "The last one of this year I reckon. The snow'll be too deep in a week or so." He winked at Jacob. "I spec I'll have to bide at home with the missus and the brat for a few months."

Jacob laughed at him. He knew he was only kidding; Mr. Sablonski adored both his missus and Dick. "Did you see any Injins?"

"Yeah, I did," Mr. Sablonski said absently. Jacob saw he was staring at him oddly and he reached over and pulled up Jacob's sleeve to expose a large angry bruise. He stared at it for a long moment, and then asked quietly, "How'd you get the bruise, Jacob?"

Jacob didn't know what to say. He stared hard at the horse's tail, and whispered, "I don't know."

"The vile fat ogre!"

Jacob stared at the tinker in alarm. He had never seen him angry before; had never even heard him raise his voice. It frightened him a bit but also made him feel very good. Mr. Sablonski was angry on his behalf.

"It doesn't matter," he said.

Mr. Sablonski considered him. "No, Jacob," he said, "it does matter. It matters a great deal." He stared down the road toward the mill. The muscles of his jaw were working, and his hands holding the reins were like iron.

They rode on in silence for a few moments, and then Jacob heard him say quietly, "But there is not a solitary thing I can do to change it." The tinker was still staring at his horse. "The law says you've got to serve him, and serve him you must. And it'd take a lot more than a few bruises to prove he was mistreating you, I expect."

He was silent for a few more paces, and then turned to look Jacob in the eye. "But if he gets too bad, Jacob, I want you to come to me." His eyes grew as hard as stones. "And as God is my witness, Jacob, I'll do what I can to help you."

34

Jacob did not know what to say, and so merely nodded.

They had come to Mr. Sablonski's drive and he pulled up the wagon. "You'd best walk the rest of the way, Jake. I fear getting any closer to the mill at the moment." He grinned. "I might just do something I'd later regret."

Jacob nodded and climbed down. "I thank you for the ride, Mr. Sablonski."

"You're welcome, Jacob." He leaned from the seat to grip Jacob's shoulder, and waited for him to look him in the eye. "I meant what I said. I want you to come to me if he gets too bad."

Jacob was having trouble holding back his tears, and didn't trust himself to speak, so he just nodded and turned to run the rest of the way to the mill.

He heard the voice of Mr. O'Connel before he had even entered the courtyard and his heart sank. *Dick was right. He told me I would not like Mr. O'Connel, and I don't. I wonder if anyone likes him.*

The man seemed to take an evil pleasure in ridiculing and humiliating the miller. Sometimes Jacob suspected he invented a reason to come to the mill for that very purpose. *Does he treat everyone thusly? If he does, how can he have any friends?*

Maybe he doesn't have any.

But Jacob suspected Mr. O'Connel did not treat everyone as he did the miller. He doubted most men would tolerate it as did the miller.

Jacob could tell by the tone of his voice that Mr. O'Connel was enjoying himself again. He could afford to; he never had to pay for his indignities.

Some one else would, as soon as the bully left. Jacob knew from sad experience it would be either he or the missus; likely whichever of them attracted the miller's attention first.

He slipped into the courtyard hoping to make it into the barn while the men were in the mill. He was almost there when he noticed the missus frantically removing clothes from the line. His sense of mercy wrestled with his desire for safety, but he finally hurried over to help her.

The clothes were soon removed, and she picked up the basket and scurried into the house as Jacob hurried to the barn. They had both been fortunate. Mr. O'Connel and the miller were still in the mill.

He started milking one of the cows. He wondered who would be beaten that evening, himself or the missus. Now that both had succeeded avoiding attention, it was hard to predict. He hoped it would be the missus. He felt guilty for that hope, but his muscles were already sore; he didn't need bruises on top of them.

He heard the men come out of the mill and cross the courtyard. Then a happy thought occurred to him; perhaps neither he nor the missus would be beaten. Perhaps his moving the fence would sate the brute's wrath.

The fence was the boundary between the miller's farm land and that of Mr. O'Connel. Moving the fence had stolen land from Mr. O'Connel. That had been why he had been commanded to do it after all the harvests were done, but before the ground froze solid. By the time Mr. O'Connel visited his farm next spring, there would be little evidence of the theft and he would be unlikely to notice it.

But Jacob then heard Mr. O'Connel say, "I sure wonder what yer father would say if'n he could see what yeh've done with the mill. If'n I recollect rightly he never held with these newfangled ways." He paused and Jacob imagined him standing and staring about himself as he often did. "Reckon he'd'a kept the buildings a shade better shape too."

Jacob's heart sank. Whenever the fat miller was reminded of his father, Jacob knew he could expect to be beaten, and thoroughly.

His rage and hatred surged, and he turned from the cow to beat his fists in impotent fury against the floor. *Some day--some day, I shall be strong; I'll never be beaten again. I shall repay the miller for every bruise. Someday, somehow, I shall find a way to make him pay!*

'The miller' was too mild; he needed something stronger. He remembered what Mr. Sablonski had called him; 'vile ogre' but that was still too tame. He needed something vulgar but suitable . . . *Freveln misthode;* he liked that.

But he then heard his grandpa's voice in his head. His grandpa had survived a pogrom in Austria when many Jews had not. He had done so by his meekness and submission. "Be patient," Jacob remembered him saying, "do not anger them; do what they say. Yes, they may beat you; they may steal from you, they may humiliate you, but you shall live to see another day. And who knows what God shall give you on that day? The important thing is to survive."

Jacob sank to the straw in despair. He resigned himself to his fate. It was only a beating; it would soon be over. *I must submit. I must not anger him; it is the way to survive.*

7 Despair

October, 1764

"Get on with yeh, yeh old nag,"

Jacob winced as the miller lashed the poor mare, Molly, time and again.

"Move, I tell yeh, move." And another lash fell.

"She's doing the best she can," Jacob wanted to yell. He wished he could snatch the reins from the brute's hand, and lash him. Let him see how he liked it. But all he did was put his shoulder to the back of the buckboard, and try to help the horse move it from the rut it had dropped into. *If the great oaf would help lift and push, we'd get moving a whole lot easier and quicker.*

Finally the buckboard heaved up from the rut, and they continued slowly home with the miller continuing to vent his wrath upon the sorry mare with curses and yells. Jacob was sorry for the mare but glad the wrath was not directed at him.

But his anger, never far from the surface, seethed and threatened to consume him. He scowled at the beast stomping along before him abusing the mare. *Freveln misthode.*

The expletive vented his emotions even though he had not uttered it aloud. He laughed to himself. He liked calling the beleibt bastard that ruled his life a freveln misthode. He had even said it aloud once or twice in the oaf's hearing. The great ox did not understand German. *God help me if he ever finds out what it means.* But he wasn't going to stop calling him that; it was the only vent he had for his emotions.

He also liked how the two words flowed off his tongue. The fact that 'misthode' was somewhat obscene was an added incentive.

When they entered the courtyard of the mill, the miller told Jacob to care for the mare, and unload the buckboard, and went into the house. Jacob drove the mare to beside the mill, and unhitched the poor animal. When she was free of the fils, she rested her sorrowful head upon his shoulder, and sighed.

"I know, Molly," he said, rubbing her neck and scratching behind her ear. "I know. Yeh didn't deserve to be yelled at like that. Yeh were doing the best yeh could." His anger boiled. "He should have been the one to be lashed, not yeh."

She sighed again, and leaned harder; she was getting quite heavy. Besides, Jacob did not want their master to see them standing idle, so he lifted her head off.

"Come on." She followed him to the barn, and waited patiently for him to remove the harness. He then brushed her down which he knew she liked, and put her in the stall she shared with the other horse, Bobby.

It is too bad we hadn't been driving Bobby. The old misthode wouldn't have lashed him like he did Molly; Bobby wouldn't have tolerated it. No one lashed him; they'd get a swift kick or, if he could reach them, a vicious bite. Even the misthode treated Bobby with respect.

Jacob knew he had to get the buckboard unloaded, so he reluctantly left the horses and began. He could plainly hear the old man berating the missus although he could not hear her replies.

"Yeh haven't even started supper? What the blazes yeh been doing?"

"I know what time it is!"

"So milk the critter."

"Never mind; I'll do it myself."

The door slammed open, and the man stomped out. "Jacob, grab a bucket and get the missus some milk. I'll empty the buckboard."

Jacob hurried to obey. He left the miller muttering, "I don't know why I gotta do everything around here."

Jacob was glad he could milk the cow. No matter how carefully he might have emptied the buckboard, and packed the goods away in their proper shelves, he knew his master would have found something for which to berate him. It was hard to screw up milking a cow.

When he carried the full bucket to the house, he could hear the brute again attacking his wife.

"Hell and perdition, would yeh watch what yer doing? Look how yeh've seared that meat!"

Jacob knocked on the door.

"Miranda, get the milk. That meat aint fit for a dog."

The door was opened, and Miranda took the bucket. Jacob stood mesmerized by the sight of his master railing and threatening as his tiny wife cowered before him like a mouse cornered by a cat.

"No I won't cut off the burnt part; cut another slice."

"Yes, Martin."

"See yeh don't burn it this time."

"I'll try."

"No. No, blast yeh. Give me that knife. Can't yeh do anything?"

"I'm sorry, Martin."

The brute snatched the knife from her, and shoved her against a shelf. There was the clatter of pans and plates and, like an animal, he went into a frenzy, threw the knife away, and, pinning her into the corner, began to rain blows upon her cowering body.

Miranda slammed the door in Jacob's face. He turned away sickened at what he had witnessed. But it had not only been the miller's abuse which had shocked him; it had been the behavior of the missus. He suddenly despised her.

He knew she had only been trying to placate her husband and avoid provoking a beating, but her meek submission had been revolting.

He returned to the barn as depressed as he could remember ever having been. He knew the reason her behavior had so repulsed him. It was because it mirrored his own behavior when faced with the miller's wrath. He had never felt so ashamed of himself.

"But what else can I do?" he asked himself. "I have to submit if I am to survive."

It had been how he had been taught to react; to obey, submit, and be meek and appeasing. Often his anger had flared and he had been tempted to react accordingly, but always he would remember his grandpa's cautions. "Be patient, Jacob. Just do what they tell you; do not make them angry. It is better to be tolerant and safe, than to arouse animosity." And the Dutchman's advice; "It does not matter what should be; only what is."

So he would swallow his wrath and submit; try to appease. He hated himself for acting so, but it was the way to survive.

"Grandpa Meier endured persecution," Jacob had told himself, "and he survived. He taught me how to survive." He had been thankful for what his grandpa had taught him. "If he could do it, then so can I."

So Jacob had endured, he had tolerated, he had survived. But walking to the barn, he almost wished he had not. He wished he was dead.

He went into the horses stall again. Before he had gone to comfort Molly; now he needed her to comfort him. The horses sensed his mood, and came to nuzzle him. He leaned against Bobby, and allowed the tears to flow.

The horse's strength sustained and steadied him. "Good old Bobby," he said. "I wish I could be like yeh." The horse nuzzled his shoulder and neck, and he turned to find the patient eye of the gelding staring at him.

"Why can't yeh be," it seemed to ask.

Yes, why can't I be? He stood straighter. *Why can't I be like Bobby? Why shouldn't I be?*

Because the freveln misthode would kill me. I'm not as strong as Bobby.

Even Bobby was occasionally beaten and, when he was, was beaten exceedingly brutally. Jacob traced the scars which crisscrossed the horse's chest and back.

But he was not abused as often as was Molly. Jacob reached out and scratched the mare behind her ear. She was almost as strong as Bobby, but she was as meek and submissive as the missus and he. As much as Jacob liked Molly, he was disgusted by her. It was not Bobby's strength which made the difference; it was his spirit.

Could . . . Jacob hardly dared to think it. *Could it be that my master would respect me like he does Bobby if I demanded it?* He shook his head. He did not believe anything he could do would ever make his master respect him.

Far more likely it would throw him into a rage, and he would beat me worse than he ever has before. He was afraid to try.

But could acting boldly really cause the freveln misthode to beat him worse than he sometimes already did? He did not see how it could; there had been times the oaf had flown into such a rage Jacob had been afraid he would kill him. *How could he beat me worse?*

His shame and despair coalesced into a cold rage which hardened into a resolution. He would no longer be a Molly; he would be a Bobby. He was tired of being meek.

Grandpa Meier's cautions echoed in his head, but he refused to listen.

Grandpa Meier may have seen many things, but he never saw America. His ways may have been wise in Amsterdam, but

42

*this is Philadelphia. I must do what I must to survive here . . .
now.*

His stomach rumbled. He realized he was very hungry. He
wondered if anyone would remember to feed him. It was not
uncommon for them to forget; he did not look forward to spending
another hungry night.

He considered Bobby. *What would Bobby do? If he was a
boy, that is.* He did not know, but he knew the horse would not
tolerate spending the night hungry. He would complain until
someone fed him. Jacob knew he had to go to the house and ask
for his food.

No, not ask; demand.

He left the horses, and strode toward the house. But the
closer he got to the house, the more his courage seeped away. He
wished he could have brought Bobby with him. He could still hear
the master grumbling, but fortunately he no longer seemed to be
yelling. He stood on the stoop, and tried to regain his resolve.

He finally reached his hand to the door and tried to rap
upon it demandingly, but it came out a timid tap even he could
hardly hear. He tapped harder. The door opened. He was
relieved to see it was the missus.

"Please missus, may I . . . that is . . . could I . . . have my
supper?"

The missus glanced over her shoulder at her husband, who
scowled and nodded. She went to the stew pot, ladled a generous
portion into his bowl, and brought it to Jacob.

The one good thing about the miller, Jacob thought with a
grin, *is he always has plenty of stew; usually pretty good stew
too.* The misthode denied himself little in the way of good food.
And, as was usual with families in the village, any leftover food
was dumped into the small cauldron which hung by the fire. There
it would combine with whatever was already in the cauldron. The
heat from the fire would keep the food from spoiling, a bit of water
added from time to time would keep it from burning, and a ready
made stew was always available for a quick meal with no
preparation. It was this stew upon which Jacob lived. Thus, the
better the fat ox ate, eventually the better he ate.

He took the bowl, thanked the missus, and returned to the barn. He had gotten his supper; he would not have to spend a hungry night, but he was still dissatisfied with his conduct.

He had wanted to act with boldness, not timidity. If he was bold, the consequences might prove unpleasant, but he would at least be proud of himself. He ate his stew determined it would be different in the morning; he would then be bold. He began to plan his actions.

He removed his clothes and burrowed into the straw. His clothes were the same with which he had arrived at the mill; they were now so threadbare and small he had to take great care not to rip them. He was afraid to sleep in them.

He realized he should not tolerate wearing the rags; he was sure Bobby wouldn't if he were a boy. But what could he do? Slowly a plan began to evolve and he fell asleep both anticipating and dreading the morning.

8 Defiance

October, 1764

He awoke just as the eastern horizon was beginning to brighten. His master always came with a breakfast as soon as the sun arose. He would then issue his orders for the day.

That morning Jacob did not wait for his master to come, but went boldly to the house door and knocked upon it. When his master came and saw it was Jacob, his face turned crimson and he reached out to grab him by his collar.

"What have yeh done now? What is wrong?"

Jacob forced himself to look him in the eye. "I have done nothing," he said." But I have come to tell yeh I require new clothes; these are rags." To accentuate his point he stepped away from the brute and allowed most of his shirt to rip off and remain in the freveln misthode's hand.

The stupid oaf stared at the rag in his hand with a slack jaw. Jacob had to struggle not to laugh.

When the great ox finally looked up, Jacob was ready. He stood before him with crossed arms and declared, "I'll take my bowl of food, if yeh please, and return to the barn. After I eat, I shall do the morning chores and bring yeh the milk when I am done. But I shall be unable to go out in public until yeh provide me with new garments."

He turned upon his heel and returned to the barn fully aware that he was showing a considerable portion of his buttock. He had deliberately split his pants. He knew the miller might be willing for him to be seen with half a shirt, but not even he would dare allow him to be seen with such pants, and they could not be mended.

To his satisfaction, before he had finished milking the three cows, the loathsome Miranda appeared with a set of clothes. He saw at a glance that they were far from new; in fact he recognized them as having belonged to the neighbor's son, but they were far larger and in better repair than his old. He took them gratefully.

Miranda said, "Father told me to bring yer old clothes so they can be burned, so give 'em to me." She did not give him the dignity of turning her back, but stood staring at him with a leer.

Jacob refused to give her the satisfaction of shaming him. He stood boldly staring at her as he stripped off his rags and calmly donned his new garments with slow deliberation. He was pleased to see her blush and look away uncertainly.

She gathered up his rags, and ran from the barn.

Jacob watched her go and laughed, and then returned to his cow. Being bold was working out just fine.

He suddenly realized he had neglected to wait for his bowl of food. When he had finished milking, he took the full buckets to the house and again knocked upon the door.

When the freveln misthode answered it, he refused to look Jacob in the eye, but accepted the buckets without a word. He seemed uneasy and unsure of himself.

Jacob realized with a shock that he was reacting to him as he normally did to other men. He pressed his advantage by demanding his breakfast, and asking what his tasks were to be for the day.

The man handed him his bowl and listed several tasks, and Jacob nodded and returned to the barn. He could not believe the change he had wrought.

It did not last long. Before evening the freveln misthode was back to his loud, belligerent self; berating Jacob with a multitude of insults and curses.

But although he had been visited by Mr. O'Connel who had dealt him his usual abuse, he did not beat Jacob. Jacob realized with awe his master was afraid to touch him.

The great brute was a coward.

9 Ice Packing

January, 1765

Jacob snuggled up against the cow he was milking, and tried to forget how cold he was. His master had not supplied him with winter clothes. His master seemed to think his summer garments were sufficient since he no longer required him to work out of the barn, but the past week had been so cold even the barn was frigid.

Even burrowing deep into the straw of his stall he had shivered violently the entire night. It had not helped that his master had forgotten to feed him the evening before. Cold and hungry he had lain as miserable as he could remember ever having been. He had almost wished he would die.

It would serve the old miller right if I did die.

At that moment the door of the barn opened to admit Dick.

Jacob jumped up from his stool with a delighted gasp. It had been months since he had seen his neighbor and friend. "What are you doing here?"

Dick feigned disappointment. "I . . . I'm sorry. You didn't want me to come?"

Jacob dropped to the stool and, seizing a teat, sent a stream of milk into Dick's face. He laughed to see him sputter, and said, "That's what you get for teasing me. You know how happy I am to see you. But why are you here?"

Dick wiped his face, and laughed back. "Good aim! My father and I came to ask the miller to rent you to us again."

A surge of pure joy swept over Jacob, but was as quickly quenched by despair. He stared down at the pail of milk. "I cannot go, I have no warm clothes." When Dick did not answer, he glanced up to find him glaring at him.

"I know you do not," his friend said. "But we have brought you everything you shall need." He scowled. "Not to keep, you understand." He stared at Jacob sadly for a long moment. "I wish we could let you keep them, but we can't. But we can let you use them for today." The boy grinned. "Hurry up with that milking so you can try them on."

"Try them on?" Jacob asked. "But . . . we don't know yet if the miller shall allow me to go with you."

"Ha," Dick snorted. "He'll allow it. What else could he have you do that would earn him two shillings in one day?"

"Two shillings! Your father is going to pay two shillings for me?" Jacob stared at Dick in disbelief. "What could I do that would be worth two shillings?"

"You're going to pack ice," Dick said with a grin. "You and I both are."

"Pack ice? What does that mean?"

"You'll see. Hurry and finish the milking."

Jacob hurried, and soon was trying on the garments Dick and his father had brought for him. There was a long coat, canvas boots, a hat, and a long scarf. They were all a little large except the scarf, but they were very warm, and Jacob closed his eyes and basked in their comfort.

The door was thrown open, and a blast of arctic wind swept in which Jacob hardly noticed, but it also admitted the ugly hulk of his master. He scowled at the sight of Jacob in his warm garments, but only said curtly, "Yeh'll serve Mr. Sablonski today," and withdrew, taking the milk buckets with him.

"Didn't I tell you?" Dick said with a grin. He punched Jacob in the arm. "You're with us for the day."

Jacob grinned back. The day had become a wonderful day.

Mr. Sablonski drove them to a building built into the side of a hill beside a large frozen pond. When he led them inside, Jacob was surprised to discover how large it was. It went into the hillside quite a ways, and the walls where he could see them were almost two feet thick. In the center was a huge pile of sawdust.

Mr. Sablonski handed a long rake to each of the boys. "Lay into it," he ordered. "Dick, you tell Jake what needs to be done." He smiled at them. "If you hurry, you should be finished in time to come out and watch the cutting for a spell. Just mind you stay far back from the hole." He turned and left.

Jacob stared at Dick. "Watch the cutting? What is that?"

"You'll see," Dick answered. He ran over to the pile of sawdust. "Come on! We've got to spread a layer of sawdust six inches thick over the whole floor and then move what's left of the pile into the far corner." He took off his coat, hat, and scarf. "Take yours off too. You'll be plenty hot without them."

Jacob did so, and they were soon making the sawdust fly. It was hard work, and Dick was right; Jacob was soon more than warm enough. It was a large floor too, and then the pile had to be moved into the corner. Jacob wondered why the pile had not been made in the corner in the first place, but was afraid to ask. Long before they had finished, his muscles ached. He was very glad when they were finally done.

He wanted to collapse and rest, but Dick would not allow him to do so.

"Come on. This is our chance to watch them cut the ice. We'll be far too busy later." He hurried over to don his garments, and Jacob followed him.

At first they were stiflingly hot, but as soon as they left the building he was glad he had them. Although the sight which met his eye made him forget about the cold.

Half a dozen men had chopped a large triangular hole in the center of the pond ice, and Mr. Sablonski and two other men were each busily pumping a cross cut saw up and down to cut a long straight line from each side of it.

Dick led Jacob carefully over to his father.

Mr. Sablonski paused when he saw them, wiped his brow, and grinned at them. "What do you think, Jake?"

Jacob stared at him, and then gaped at the line he was cutting. He had never heard of people cutting ice like this. He wondered why they were. He looked back at Mr. Sablonski who was waiting for an answer. He did not know what to say, but finally said, "That looks like hard work."

"Ah, it's not so bad," Dick's father said. "At least I'm the man on top of the ice."

Jacob's jaw dropped. He knew it took two men to operate a cross cut saw, one on each end, but surely . . . He peered at the cold blue ice. There couldn't be a man on the other end of the saw . . . could there?

Mr. Sablonski roared with laughter, and began to pump the saw again.

Jacob grinned at him. He liked it when Mr. Sablonski teased him; it made him feel good. He looked again at the cut he had made in the ice. "How do you make it so straight?" he asked.

Mr. Sablonski did not pause in his rhythm but answered, "Years of practice, my lad. Years of practice." He stopped cutting and, working the saw along the cut, returned to the hole in the ice.

Jacob and Dick followed him, but he would not allow them to come too close to the edge. They watched as he began a new cut a foot and a half from the first. Jacob was amazed to watch him keep the new cut exactly parallel.

In a surprisingly short time the new cut was the same length as the old, and Mr. Sablonski again worked the saw back to the hole, but this time pulled it out and laid it aside. He grabbed up a long pole and an ax, called to the remaining five men, and returned to his saw cut ends while the five hurried to the point of the hole opposite his side.

Jacob wondered what they were all doing, but just stood with Dick and watched.

Mr. Sablonski cracked the ice between the cuts with the ax, and Jacob saw he had made a long thin slab of ice which popped up to float several inches above the surrounding ice. Mr. Sablonski took the pole, and pushed the slab out into the hole and into the corner opposite it. There one man used an ax to crack off blocks a foot and a half square while two others, at either end of an enormous pair of tongs, hoisted them from the water and placed them on a sled.

Jacob wanted to continue watching, but Dick nudged him.

"Come on. We have to go back inside. They'll be bringing the ice in a moment."

They hurried inside, and stripped off their coats, hats, and scarves. And sure enough, the remaining two men soon appeared with the load of ice. With another set of tongs, the men unloaded the ice blocks, and placed them in a row six inches from the far wall and three inches apart.

They then hurried back for more while Jacob, following Dick's example, grabbed an armful of sawdust from the pile, and quickly packed it into the space between the blocks. Barely had the two boys finished, when a new batch of blocks awaited them.

Jacob soon got his pace, and they began to finish well before the new blocks arrived, but they got no opportunity to rest, for they also had to spread a three inch layer of sawdust on top of the blocks. They were unable to keep up with the men.

Before he knew it, the entire floor, except where the pile was, was filled, and the men began to lay another tier. He and Dick raced to finish stuffing the cracks of the first, spread the layer on top of them, and hurried to begin the second tier.

Jacob was surprised when Dick told him not to put a new layer of sawdust on the second tier; just stuff the cracks. He wondered why, but was too busy to ask. He discovered why when the men, having finished laying the blocks of the second tier, grabbed shovels and began spread a layer upon the ice while he and Dick hurried to stay ahead of them.

Then they grabbed shovels also, and helped the men move the huge pile of sawdust into a new corner on top of the ice. They left a six inch layer on the floor, and the men left to return with new blocks which the boys hurried to pack. Soon the hole had been filled with its two tiers of ice and a third tier began to fill the floor.

The grueling pace continued until Jacob was exhausted. He had lost count of the number of tiers they had made. He was ashamed he and Dick could never quite keep up with the pace; always the men had to help them with the last of a pair of tiers. He was afraid he was not earning his two shillings.

Finally the men announced it was time for a break; it was time to cat. Jacob was starving. He hoped Mr. Sablonski had brought plenty of food.

But, to his surprise, a wagon of women had appeared, and they began to bring platters of food into the building until Jacob was staring at an amazing feast. And Mr. Sablonski assured him he was free to eat as much as he desired just like the others. He was not slow to comply; it had been a very long time since he had eaten such food.

He overheard one of the two men who had brought in the ice blocks say to Mr. Sablonski, "Yeh brought us a right spry boy there, Gus." Jacob glanced up surprised. He had thought Mr. Sablonski's name was Gustaf. But then he guessed 'Gus' was the American name for 'Gustaf' just like 'Dick' was the name for 'Richard'. At least 'Gus' he could understand; he still wondered why they called boys whose name was Richard, 'Dick'.

Then he realized the man had been talking about him, and his jaw dropped. He had thought he had done poorly, but he saw the other ice man nod.

"Aye," the man said, "I aint never seen his match; lessen it was your Dick there. We had to hustle to keep ahead of 'em."

Mr. Sablonski was smiling, and he winked at Jacob. "Yeh'd go many a mile to find a finer boy, I spec."

Jacob felt himself blushing and, staring down upon the pie before him, attacked it fiercely. The men approved of him and . . . Mr. Sablonski liked him. He could feel the waves of affection flow over him. He had to struggle to contain the tears which threatened to spill. He finished the pie and realized he did not know what kind of pie it had been.

He stole a glance at Mr. Sablonski, and saw he was engaged in a debate about politics. He was glad. He determined, as exhausted as he felt, he would work even faster that afternoon. He would not give the men reason to rejudge his value.

He would die before he would let Mr. Sablonski down.

To his relief he found he was able to keep his resolve; he and Dick kept pace with the supply of blocks quite well. He began to feel a bit proud of himself until Dick pointed out that, as the tiers mounted, the men had a great deal more labor to bring the blocks. They could not help but slow the pace.

"Besides," Dick said, "the men are getting tired too."

Soon the men no longer spread every other layer or helped the boys move the pile, but that was all right for the pile was greatly diminished and easily moved.

Finally the ice was so high the men had to squat to move in another tier, and Jacob and Dick spread a foot thick layer of sawdust upon it, the stair stepping hole which had been left so the new ice could be brought in was gradually filled, and the job was done.

Jacob was surprised to see the sun was still up when he left the building. It had felt much later than that. He was very tired and glad to tell the other men goodbye, and climb into Mr. Sablonski's wagon for the ride home.

"What are you going to do with all that ice?" he asked as they rode.

"It belongs to a merchant in Philly," Mr. Sablonski said. "He has dozens of similar ice houses up the coast all the way past New York Colony. He'll load it up in insulated ships and send it all over the world." He grinned back at Jacob. "Some of that ice you packed will end up cooling the tea for the governor of India sometime next summer."

Jacob's jaw dropped. He wondered if Mr. Sablonski was teasing him again, but he saw he was serious.

It filled him with wonder. He wished he could travel all that way with the ice. He had heard stories about India: cats as big as horses, other animals as large as houses which were so strong they could lift an entire tree with their noses, and mountains covered in ice which never melted. He did not know if he believed those stories, but he wished he could see them.

Far too soon, he saw they were nearing the mill. The wonderful day was nearly over.

But before it was, Mr. Sablonski leaned back and pressed a shilling into Jacob's hand. "It is yours. You earned it. The merchant paid three shillings for a day's packing, and I only paid the miller two. But he was satisfied with the two, and he does not need to know you earned three. You understand? This shilling is yours."

Jacob stared at the coin, and then at Mr. Sablonski. "I can't keep this. It belongs to my master."

"My great aunt Nanny's fanny it does," the man snorted. "The law says you owe him your labor. It says nothing regarding your money. I tell you he rented you to me for two shillings of his own free will; that is all which is his due. The third shilling is your own."

"But," Jacob said, "since I was rented to you, the shilling belongs to you."

Mr. Sablonski stopped the wagon abruptly and turned to glare at Jacob. "I said, 'the shilling is yours,' and I'll brook no further arguing. You put that coin away somewhere safe. If I find that . . . master of yours gets it, I'll be mighty displeased. You hear me?"

Jacob nodded dumbly, and the man smiled.

"You did a good job today, Jake. I'm proud of you. By rights that merchant ought to give you an extra shilling; you and Dick both." He turned, and started his horse again. "I just may tell him so, next time I see him."

He pulled up at the gate of the mill, and let Jacob off. "Good day to yeh, Jake."

Jacob watched them begin to pull away, but then realized he was still wearing the winter garments, and began to strip them off calling, "Wait. Yeh forgot these."

Mr. Sablonski glanced back. "Yeh may keep them until next time."

"Next time?" Jacob asked hopefully.

"Aye," Mr. Sablonski called back over his shoulder. "The merchant has two other ice houses nigh. Iffen this weather holds we'll fill another this Saturday."

This Saturday, Jacob thought. The thought of spending another day so soon with Dick and his father filled him with joy. But then he realized Saturday was only two days hence. Could he work that hard again so soon?

10   The Missus

November, 1765

Another year was winding down; it would soon again be winter.

Jacob's master called him over to where he sat making entries into his account book. After a moment he looked up and said, "It'll freeze soon. I'll have yeh move the fence another fifteen feet on the morrow."

Jacob knew he meant the stone fence separating his farm from that of Mr. O'Connel, stealing another acre or so. Although Jacob had moved the fence on his master's orders both of the previous autumns, the foolish bully had never noticed. Yet, despite Jacob's dislike for Mr. O'Connel and the fact that he was only obeying his master, the practice had begun to weigh upon his conscience.

Yet what could he do?

He was no longer the meek frightened child he had once been. Since the day he had forced himself to demand new garments he had practiced being bold until boldness had become a habit. By acting bold he had developed a self assurance which he had soon discovered others found intimidating, particularly his master. Their relationship, such as it was, had been transformed. The bolder and more self assured Jacob had grown, the more his master had come to hate but also fear him. No longer did Jacob quake at his wrath and no longer was he beaten.

Yet Jacob had never disobeyed his master's orders. Unjust though it was, the law said he owed his master another nineteen years of servitude and the law had very effective means to enforce that debt. He knew better than to give his master cause to call the magistrate.

But, with a start, he realized this was one matter regarding which his master could not appeal to the magistrate.

He grinned at the oaf, and said proudly, "I shall not."

For a moment his master did not notice his refusal, but continued to list the tasks he wanted Jacob to do. Then he looked up with a scowl.

"What did yeh say?"

"I said, 'I shall not,'" Jacob answered calmly.

For a moment his master was livid, but then his eyes narrowed and he seemed almost pleased. "Refusing to obey a master be a punishable offense," he said. He turned, and called over his shoulder to his daughter. "Miranda, go for the magistrate."

The girl smirked at Jacob, and hurried out the gate.

Jacob cleared his throat. "Call her back."

"Ah! Singin' a new tune, are yeh?" crowed his master. "I thought yeh might." His face grew cold. "Well it is too late for yeh. I've had enough of yer haughty ways. I'll see yeh publicly flogged, I shall." He grinned. "Mayhap they'll add a few months to yer service."

"Aye," Jacob said quietly. "But what shall the magistrate do when he hears what yeh've ordered me to do?"

His master jumped and stared at him. Jacob held his gaze and asked, "What is the penalty for moving a border fence, do yeh know?"

The master's face was crimson and his eyes bulged. He raised his fist as if to beat Jacob, but he lowered it again. "Be yeh threatening me?"

"No," Jacob replied amiably, "I only am pointing out why yeh don't want Miranda to fetch the magistrate." He gazed at the empty gate and back at his master. "I'd stop her were I yeh."

The master was so angry spit was oozing from the corners of his mouth, but he jumped up and ran after his daughter.

* * * *

Late that night Jacob awoke and heard the misthode and the missus arguing. It was not unusual to hear the misthode yelling but, for the very first time he could remember, he heard the missus. He could not quite make out what either of them was saying, but he lay amazed at her daring. He was impressed by her and silently cheered her on, hoping she would not end up beaten. He fell back asleep before they had finished arguing.

Very early the next morning the master came to the barn, said, "Yeh'll do as the missus tells yeh," and, turning upon his heel, strode across the courtyard to the gate and disappeared.

Jacob stood staring after him for several moments astounded. He had never been ordered to obey the missus; always before when the master had been absent he had been commanded to obey Miranda.

He found himself eager to get his orders from the missus; in all the years he had spent in service to her family he had hardly spoken with her. But he waited until after the sun had risen and he had milked the cows.

When he knocked upon the door, she answered it, took the buckets without a word, and carried them into the kitchen. Miranda was nowhere to be seen.

"I . . . I am to do as yeh command," Jacob called after her.

She turned with a gentle smile. Her head rose and her shoulders squared. For the first time Jacob saw she must once have been an attractive woman.

"Come in Jacob," she invited. She pointed her chin at the table where two plates were sitting. "Sit yerself at the table. I'll be back presently."

She's inviting me into the house? Jacob had never before been invited into the house. He entered cautiously and sat himself on the end of one of the benches flanking the table. He tried not to stare at the fine furnishings surrounding him; he had not seen such opulence even in Amsterdam. He ran his hand across the polished surface of the table. It was solid oak, and the chair at its head was cherry.

The missus returned carrying a platter of pancakes and set it upon the table. She glanced at where he was seated. "No, no, Jacob, sit yerself here." She patted the table beside one of the plates.

Jacob slid himself wonderingly to the plate as the missus went back to the kitchen and returned with a plate loaded with bacon and a pitcher of water. She set them down and seated herself before the other plate. He stared at her trying not to allow his jaw to drop. Did she really intend for him to eat such food? At her table? With her?

She smiled at Jacob and asked, "Would yeh thank the Lord for our food, Jacob?"

He stared at the plate in confusion for a moment and then looked her in the eye. "I . . . I'm a Jew."

There was a momentary flit of something, he was not certain what emotion it was, across her face, and then she smiled again. "Jews thank God for their food, do they not?" He nodded, and she said, "Then please do so."

She bowed her head and he did also. What was he to say? Fortunately the prayer his father had always intoned before their meals came to him and he repeated it. He glanced up and blushed. He realized he had prayed in German. He should have translated it into English.

But the missus only nodded and said graciously, "Thank yeh, Jacob." Her eyes seemed far away. "My father always thanked the Lord before our meals. I have so . . ."

She returned to the present and smiled sadly. "Thank yeh, Jacob." She briskly pushed the platter of pancakes to him. "Help yerself. Oh! I've forgotten the syrup." She jumped up and scurried into the kitchen.

Jacob carefully took two of the cakes. He still found it hard to believe he was to be allowed to eat them.

"Gracious, Jacob," the missus exclaimed as she returned with the syrup. "yeh need far more than that." And seizing his fork, she speared four more cakes and flipped them onto his two and then liberally poured syrup upon them. She also scooped up a liberal quantity of bacon and crowded them beside the cakes. She then sat and ordered, "Now eat."

He stared at the piles of food and then at her. She was filling her own plate but, without even glancing at him, again commanded him to eat. He cut into the cakes and took a large bite; they were delicious.

Together they silently ate. After a bit he began to worry; it was wonderful to be fed in such a manner, but he wondered what price the missus would be forced to pay when the master heard of it. He was sure he would not be pleased. And that loathsome Miranda would be sure to tell him. He finally asked, "Where is Miranda?"

The missus glanced up. Again emotions he could not read flitted across her face and then she stared back at her plate and murmured, "She is with 'er father."

Too soon the meal was finished, and the missus sat seeming unsure what to do.

"Yer to give me my orders for the day," Jacob offered.

She sat up straighter and considered him soberly for several moments. "I'll not order yeh to do anything," she finally said. "But I have a request, if yeh please."

"If . . . if I please?"

"Yes. If yeh please," she said briskly. "I'll ask yeh return the fence to its original location. Yeh know the oak on the bank of the creek?" When he had nodded she continued. "The fence is to commence there and conclude thirty feet west of where it now does. Make it run as straight as yeh can."

Jacob stared at her wondering what would happen if his master discovered him moving the fence back. He had ordered him to obey the missus. But what would happen to her?

"Will yeh do that, Jacob?" she asked.

He stared at her for a long moment. He did not know what to say. Finally he asked, "What shall the master do?"

She stared back at him but then raised her chin and smiled. "He shall do nothing. Did he not order yeh to do as I say?"

"What shall he do to yeh?"

"Not a thing." Again she smiled but this time her eyes were cold. "He does not dare."

"Why?" Jacob whispered.

The missus did not answer for several long moments; only sat staring at him. He thought he had never seen such pain and sorrow before. Then the eyes grew defiant and cold again.

"We once had another indentured boy, Jacob. His name was Andrew." Her eyes suddenly gleamed and she leaned forward and took Jacob's shoulder in her hand. "If anything ever happens to me, Jacob, I want yeh to remind the magistrate of that." She sat back. "Will yeh do that?"

He nodded.

"Good." She rose to clear the table. "Yeh may go." She smiled at him. "Thank yeh for eating with me this morning."

She was thanking him? He knew he should be thanking her. But he did not know what to say; the entire morning had been so odd. He realized she had told him to go and made his way to the door.

Just as he was opening it she called, "Jacob." He turned and again saw emotions he could not read flit rapidly across her face and disappear. Finally she said, "Have a pleasant day," and turned into the kitchen.

Jacob went to the barn thinking about his morning. He almost would not mind being indentured if she was his mistress, he thought, but she was a powerfully strange lady.

He did not look forward to moving the fence; he knew it would be hard labor. But, he grinned, the knowledge that it would be certain to infuriate his master would make it pleasant work. Yet if he was to complete the task in one day, he knew he had best hurry. Slipping out the gate, he began his jog to the farm.

He wondered what power the missus had gained over his master. What had happened to their former servant? Why had she asked him to remind the magistrate of him if something happened to her? He hoped nothing did happen.

Whatever power she had gained, he hoped she would retain.

11 Check & Mate

April, 1766

Jacob awoke with a start. For a moment he did not know what had wakened him, but he then heard the rumble of the mill wheel. Why was it engaged in the midst of the night? He began to creep to the door to look out when he heard an awful grinding and snapping noise. He realized that had been what had awakened him.

What in the world was being run through the stones, and why now? Grain did not make such noises. There it was again! He was suddenly afraid to look out the door and hurried back to his stall. Thrice more the noises sounded. Between them he could hear the familiar sound of the wheel being adjusted for a finer grind. Then all sound ceased. The mill wheel had been disengaged.

Again he felt the urge to look out and see what has happening, but he resisted it. He sensed the danger, whatever it was, was at its greatest.

Then he heard the missus cry out in pain and terror. He listened carefully for the sounds of a beating but heard only an ominous silence. He crept from the barn and dashed to hide beside the house below a window. Listening very carefully he heard the missus begging for mercy. He had never heard her beg for mercy before, even in the midst of a horrible beating, and the sound terrorized him more than the sounds of a beating would have. He heard the miller growl, "If yeh want mercy, yeh'll shut yer mouth and keep it shut." There was the sound of a door slamming, and Jacob sprinted back to the barn lest he be discovered.

He wondered what he should do. He considered running for the magistrate as the missus had told him to do if anything ever happened to her, but he did not know what had happened. Yet it was plain that whatever power the missus had gained over the miller she had lost. He buried his head in the straw and tried not to hear anything further.

In the morning his master ordered him to take the team of horses and harrow the south field of his farm. Jacob was very surprised for he knew it was far too early to harrow, but he did not argue. It was obvious the master was not in a mood to be questioned and besides, Jacob loved when he could harrow. It was easy and pleasant work which would allow him hours of solitude.

After what had transpired in the night, it was a godsend.

As he had expected, the harrow was not very effective breaking up the soil; despite the thaw of the past few days, only the top several inches were frost free. But why should he care? If his master wanted him to waste the day harrowing, he was glad to oblige him.

He noticed however that there was one patch roughly ten feet in diameter where the ground seemed to have been disturbed. The dirt was in clumps; larger and more irregular than the surrounding dirt. And when the horses walked over it, their feet sank several inches into the soil.

Jacob stopped them and peered at the strange circle carefully. He was curious why it was so. He noticed a trail of boot prints leading to it and another leading away.

He considered informing his master; perhaps it was something he should know. But he quickly discarded that idea. The last thing he wanted was to infuriate his master. Besides, the boot prints looked like they could be . . . his master's.

He wondered, could it be . . . the strange circle and the events of the night before were related? What had changed between the master and the missus in the night; what had been the power the missus had held? Why had she wielded it successfully through the winter only to now lose it?

Could it be the master had been forced to wait for the thaw before he could free himself? If so, what had been buried here? What had been ground to dust in the night? Perhaps he should ask not what, but who.

Jacob leaped from the harrow and several feet from the edge of the circle. He did not like the thought of standing upon the poor boy's grave. He was sure he knew now what had become of his master's former servant and what had been the missus' hold upon him.

But he is no longer here. The misthode removed his body and destroyed it last night. He stared at the circle in horrid fascination imagining the miller digging up the corpse. *No not corpse, bones. After four or five years there would have been only bones. Poor boy, I wonder what he was like.*

He remembered it had been a moonless night; the miller had doubtless done his loathsome deed with only a dim shielded lantern. Was it not possible, even likely, he had missed a few bones?

If Jacob could find those bones and hide them . . . might they not give him power over the beast? Who knew when he might need such leverage?

Repelled as he was at the thought of disturbing a dead boy's bones, he forced himself to begin pawing through the dirt. *I do not think Andrew would mind if he knew; he would want me to gain power over our common enemy. Perhaps I can avenge his death with them.*

It took him a good deal of time and he had to move a great deal of dirt but he was not worried about being discovered; the field was well shielded from the road and he was sure the misthode would be afraid to come near the field in the daylight. Why he was so sure he would not he could not have said, but he was sure.

Nonetheless he was about to despair of finding a bone when his fingers finally hit something long and hard. With fear and hope he dug it free and wiped the dirt from it. It was indeed a bone, just under a foot long, but it was oddly bent as if it had been broken and then welded back together.

That is exactly what it is; it was broken and not properly set. It grew together crooked. But which bone is it? Is it a human bone? Is it Andrew's bone?

He felt his own bones and compared them to the bone in his hand. It seemed too slight and short to be a leg bone. Of course he did not know how old Andrew had been when he had died. *Had been murdered,* he corrected himself. He would have to ask the missus. Still, he concluded it was an arm bone; specifically the lower bone on the outside of the arm. He realized it was lucky the bone had been broken and healed crooked; if Andrew had had a crooked arm, it would be proof it was his bone.

But what was he to do with it?

He knew exactly where in the barn he would hide it if he could get it to the barn; there was a hole along the eaves which would be very suitable and he was sure the master knew nothing of it; he was too fat to climb to it, but how was he to get the bone there?

He put the bone on the harrow and scooped the dirt back into the hole while he thought about it. Then he gently cut a long hair from Bobby's tail, tied one end around the bone and the other around his belt, and allowed it to dangle down his pants along his leg.

Having a dead boy's arm bone rubbing against his leg gave him the willies, but he forced himself to ignore it.

He stepped upon the harrow, chirped to the horses, and they recommenced their plodding. Two circuits of the field and the strange circle had been obliterated. In less than three hours the field was finished but Jacob went over it a second time. He had no desire to hurry his return to the mill; he feared passing the miller with the bone in his pants; what if he was discovered?

In the end he had to return. But he had no difficulty, and the bone was soon safely hidden in the hole.

That evening he passed close to the missus where she was gathering the dry wash from the line. He was not surprised to discover several nasty bruises on her arm and neck. She glanced furtively around; saw the miller and her daughter were both out of sight, and beckoned him over.

"Jacob," she whispered, "do yeh remember what I told yeh about the magistrate?"

He nodded.

"Well don't do it." She glanced at the mill, and then added, "It shall no longer avail."

He again nodded. Should he tell her he had found the bone? He decided not to. If the master learned the bone still existed, far from granting them power over him, it would make him far more dangerous. No. It must be kept secret from him until an appropriate time when it could be sprung upon him and Jacob did not trust the missus to keep that knowledge from him. Instead he asked, "Did Andrew have a crooked arm?"

Her eyes widened, and she stepped back. "Why . . . why would yeh ask such a thing?"

"Did he?"

She nodded, and stared into his eyes for a long moment. He said nothing but he felt very happy. He was sure he could prove the bone was Andrew's if he ever had to.

"Jacob," the missus finally whispered, as she stared into his eyes with terror. "Be careful. Be very, very careful"

He returned her stare for a long moment, and then again nodded; he intended to be. She turned back to her clothes, and he returned to the barn.

He sat in the straw, and thought over the past day and night. They had shown his master to be not only a brute but incredibly evil, but strangely Jacob did not find the knowledge as fearful as he would have thought; it instead served only to multiply his resolve to resist him.

12 The Gamble & the Loss

July, 1767

Jacob stretched, glanced at the sun, and then at the pile of sacks remaining to be mended. If he did not hurry he would not finish before his master returned and there would be hell to pay.

Although, in the more than a year which had transpired since the strange night when the mill had been run, his master had not threatened to harm him, his verbal abuse had become much worse and Jacob preferred to avoid it. Moreover he had not forgotten the missus' warning; he sensed a terrible sense of danger, even malice, pervading his master's every interaction with him.

He began to hurry. At least mending the holes in the grain sacks was easy if tedious work.

Yet a melancholy and self pity threatened to overwhelm him for this should have been a special day for him: a day of celebration. It was his birthday; July twenty third. He was thirteen. For a Jewish boy, his thirteenth birthday was a very important day. It was then he did his bar mitzvahs and become a man. Jacob remembered bar mitzvahs celebrations he had attended in his youth. But, of course, no notice of the day would be given by his master or any other.

This too had been stolen from him.

He wondered if his family still remembered him. He was sure they did; on a day like this at least. *They probably believe I am dead.*

Perhaps his grandpa Meier was lamenting once again that he had known Jacob would meet an unfortunate end; what other fate could await a son born on Tisha B'av? The twenty third of

July had always been a day of calamity for Jews. It had been then that Moses had been forced to destroy the stone tablets containing the Law because of Israel's sin; on that date, the spies had returned from exploring Canaan and Israel had failed to trust God which had resulted in their being exiled to wander the wilderness for an additional forty years. Both of the temples in Jerusalem had been destroyed on that date. On that date England had driven all Jews from Britain, and, in 1492 the Jews had been exiled from Spain. His grandpa had listed many other examples of horrible events which had occurred on that sad date.

Spain; 1492? Didn't Spain discover America in 1492? And now Jacob was exiled in America. For the first time Jacob began to think perhaps there was something in the numerology his grandpa had put such confidence in. Always before he had scoffed at it.

What he wouldn't give to sit and listen to him again. *But is my grandpa even still alive?* He did not know.

He tried to picture his family; perhaps sitting around their supper table remembering their lost son. His parents would be older now, mayhap beginning to grey. With a shock he realized Hannecke would be almost a young lady; she was two years younger than he, so she would be eleven. He tried to picture her as an eleven year old girl but was unable to do so. In his mind she was still only six.

His shoulders sagged wearily. His little sister, Margo, who had been only a tiny baby when he had been taken, would be six. A few tears escaped his eyes and ran down his cheek. He had a six year old sister, and he did not even know her.

He glanced up at the sun. It made him glad to know that same sun was shining down upon his family. It made him feel still connected to them. But he then remembered Amsterdam was almost five hours before Philadelphia. The sun had already set over Amsterdam; it was not shining upon his family.

He buried his face in the sack on his lap and allowed himself to weep.

"Yo, Jacob. Where are yeh?"

It was his master's harsh voice. Jacob threw aside the bags, and hurried into the courtyard. He found the miller standing with a young boy.

"This here is Mateo," said the master with a smirk. "He owes me seven years service and I'll have yeh take him in hand and teach him his duties." His face darkened. "I'll hold yeh responsible for any mishap." He gave the boy a hard shove and he stumbled over to Jacob's side. The miller turned upon his heel, and went into the house.

Jacob led the boy to the barn sadly. He remembered his own first night in his master's service only too well. The boy was clearly terrified, and Jacob's heart ached for him. He wondered if he had been stolen and sold like Jacob had been.

He tried to tell the boy he would be all right; he would look out for him, but he found the boy did not understand a word he said. He tried Dutch, but the boy shook his head. He tried German, and then Yiddish, with no better luck. Those were the only languages Jacob knew.

The boy said something which Jacob thought sounded a little like the Spanish he had heard on his voyage to America. Several of the crew of that horrible ship had been Spaniards and it had pleased them to teach Jacob a few Spanish words and phrases. What the boy had said had sounded like Spanish, although Jacob wasn't sure it was. Even if it was, he didn't know enough Spanish to understand it.

Still, he remembered that before he had learned English, though he had not understood the words people had said, he had always understood the tone of their voices. So he talked to the boy as he showed him the barn. He assumed the boy would share his stall, and showed him where it was.

They sat together in the straw, and Jacob wondered what else he could do to ease the boy's misery. He remembered how on his first night he had longed for a friendly touch; he had felt so alone. So he slid next to the boy, and carefully put his arm around his shoulders.

The boy stared up at him fearfully for several long moments, but then buried his head into Jacob's side and began to silently weep.

Jacob let him cry. He wondered where the boy had come from. He had black eyes set wide in a dark brown face and hair so black it shone blue. His bony little body was hard with cordlike muscles. Whatever his origin he was no stranger to hard labor.

Finally the boy fell asleep, and Jacob carefully disengaged himself and did the evening chores. He took the milk to the house, and was met by their master who gave him a bowl of stew.

"See the boy gets some," their master ordered cheerfully, and Jacob nodded and returned to the barn.

Why is he so happy? He hasn't been so happy since I don't know when.

But he did know when; the last time his master had beaten him. His master had always been happy when he had beaten him.

Jacob was afraid; not for himself, but for the boy.

But what could he do?

He awakened Mateo, and shared the stew with him. It was plain the boy was not used to eating stew with his fingers. He would learn soon enough.

He expected their master would show up very soon, but, to his surprise, he did not come. He and the boy settled into the straw side by side. Jacob's heart ached for the boy.

Yet he could not help being glad he was there. It was good to have someone to talk to even if they could not understand each other. The boy snuggled tight against Jacob's side, and was soon asleep.

The boy's confidence in him made Jacob feel good, but it also worried him. He put his arm around Mateo, and hugged him to himself. *I am only thirteen,* he reminded himself, *how can I protect him?*

He wondered how old Mateo was. He studied his face. It was hard to tell, but Jacob guessed he was maybe seven; perhaps eight.

He felt a fierce desire to protect the boy. He did not know how he could, but he determined he would try.

With that resolution he pulled more straw over the boy and himself, snuggled back with him, and fell asleep.

He awoke when Mateo was yanked from his side. The boy's cry of terror was stifled by the sickening sound of blows.

He leaped up to see Mateo writhing on the floor while their master kicked him gleefully.

He burst from the stall, and yelled, "Why are yeh beating him? He has done nothing wrong! He cannot even understand what yeh tell him. Why are yeh beating him?"

Their master leered over his shoulder, and chortled, "Because I can!" The vile man grinned. "I can do whatever I please and no one can tell me nay." He turned back to the boy.

Jacob could no longer stand it. Without a thought he drove himself against the master, and sent him stumbling to crash against the wall.

Their master rose with fiery eyes. Jacob stood between him and Mateo. "I won't let yeh beat him," he said. "Not when he has done nothing."

"And just how do yeh intend to stop me? Do yeh forget yer in my power just as he?" He sneered. "It is time yeh learned yer place. I'll call the magistrate to instruct yeh if I must. Don't make me have to."

But Jacob was not going to allow him to beat Mateo. It was time to use his knowledge of Andrew.

"Call the magistrate," he said. "I want yeh to. I have somewhat to inform him."

The man's eyes narrowed. "And of what would yeh inform him? I have a right to discipline my servants as I choose."

"Andrew."

For a moment his knowledge of the name seemed to shock the miller, but then he scoffed. "The little creature ran off nigh ten years ago. The magistrate knows that."

"But he did not run off," Jacob said evenly. "Yeh killed him and buried him in yer west field." He was watching his master and saw his words were hitting home. "Then, a year ago spring yeh dug him up and ground his bones to dust."

That communication stuck home with even greater force; the miller almost staggered, but he regained his composure and said nastily, "Yeh've no proof of any of that. Yeh said it yerself; the bones are dust."

"All but one. Yeh missed it, and I found it." Jacob crossed his arms, and glared at his master. "If yeh beat Mateo without a just cause, I'll take it to the magistrate."

The miller's face was livid, but he said quite calmly, "That shall prove nothing."

"I think it shall. How many boys have a crooked arm?" Jacob watched the blood drain from his master's face, and grinned. "Of all the bones yeh could have missed, yeh missed the one bone everyone shall know belonged to Andrew."

The master kept his eyes on Jacob, but sidled to the bin where the cow's turnips were kept. He reached in, pulled out the knife which they used to cut up the turnips, and shook it at Jacob. "Yeh're too smart for yer own good, Jacob."

Jacob looked around desperately. The only door was behind his master. He tried to run around him, but the master leaped, and caught him. Jacob struggled mightily, but was soon pinned beneath the man's massive bulk.

The ogre took his time raising the knife over him. "I hate to forfeit the sixteen years yeh still owe me," he said, "but yeh've left me no option."

Jacob wanted to close his eyes to blot out the awful face, but was unable to. *Is this what happened to Andrew? What shall it be like to die?*

The man above him suddenly grunted, and threw up his hands. The knife flew through the air to land with a thump on the floor. Their master slowly toppled forward upon him.

Jacob frantically pushed him sideways, and wriggled out from under. He saw the pitchfork embedded in their master's back. A trickle of blood was oozing from the monster's mouth. Mateo was standing staring and white faced.

Jacob picked the boy up, and turned him from the corpse. "Thank yeh," he whispered into his ear. "Thank yeh." It seemed so inadequate, but what else could he say?

13 Flight

July 24, 1767

Jacob peered into the shadows surrounding him. Each one held the terror of unseen eyes. He wished the night was darker; although the moon was hardly more than a quarter, it seemed very bright.

He resisted the desire to urge Bobby into a trot. This plodding walk was so slow; he felt it would drive him insane. He desperately needed to put miles behind him.

But haste would arouse the suspicions of any who saw them, so he allowed the horse to plod. It was unlikely he would be seen at this hour of the night, but the road was a main thoroughfare past Philadelphia and was often used by merchants even in the night. And, with his master lying dead in the back of the wagon, arousing suspicions was the last thing he desired.

He had known the moment he had seen the pitchfork in his master's back that he and Mateo must flee. No one would believe their story that he had been killed in self defense. Suddenly the idea of proving the master had killed Andrew by showing the weathered old bone had seemed absurd. Perhaps the missus would come to his defense, but he dared not assume that.

He wasn't even sure it had been self defense; Mateo had killed him, but he had done it to save Jacob. So was that self defense, since he himself had not been in mortal danger? He shook the reins angrily. It didn't matter did it? No one would believe Mateo had done it. Mateo couldn't even vouch for his story; he couldn't speak English.

No. If they did not get far away Jacob would be arrested for murder. The trial, if he even got one, would be short, and he would certainly be hung.

His first instinct had been to simply run into the night, as far and as fast as his feet could carry him. But servants who attempted to flee rarely succeeded when they fled on foot; they were far too easy to track. And he could not; would not, leave Mateo, and with him he could run neither far nor fast. So he had forced himself to be calm and think things through. It had been when his eye had fallen upon the pile of bags he had been mending the idea had come to him.

Every fall his master would take him in a wagon and make a large circuit into the surrounding countryside buying grain from the various settlements. It was a little early for such a trek, but it seemed reasonable any who saw him driving the wagon with his master in the back; seemingly asleep, would assume they were beginning their yearly trek and not question him. Mateo could be hidden under the seat.

So he had dragged his master's body into the wagon, propped it up against the side just behind the seat, and covered it with a blanket of sacks. They had then harnessed Bobby to the wagon and simply driven away. The house, thankfully, had been dark.

Jacob had been impressed by how quickly Mateo had grasped his intentions and assisted him. He had not even had to tell him to hide under the seat; the boy was obviously intelligent.

He saw a rider come around the bend before them. That he was a rider worried him; a merchant transporting goods to or from Philadelphia would certainly be driving a wagon. Why would a man be riding alone in the dead of night? He risked a glance back at his master's body. He hoped it appeared natural enough to fool anyone who might see it. When he had conceived his plan he had consoled himself with the expectation it would be too dark to see his master clearly, but the night seemed very light indeed.

He forced himself to look away, and sit slumped in the seat with the reins hanging loose in his hands as if he was half asleep. His alarm multiplied when he saw the rider was the magistrate himself.

The magistrate drew abreast, stopped, and called quietly, "Ho there, is that yeh, Jacob?"

"Yes sir, Mr. Roberts," Jacob answered. He hoped he sounded natural. "How are yeh this fine night?"

The man took off his hat, and wiped his brow. "Not so good I fear, Jacob. The Jamison gal was attacked this evening when she was bringing in her daddy's sheep. Time I got there it was dark and there was little anyone could do. I've been searching for his trail, but I give it up. I'll have to try again in the light." He glanced at Jacob. "Yeh folk have any troubles yer way?"

"No," Jacob said, hoping he sounded convincing. "Nothing's happened our way." He just wanted to get rid of the magistrate, but he forced himself to ask, "Be the Jamison gal all right?"

"Naw. Naw she aint." The magistrate shook his head. "She's hurt bad. I spec she'll pull through all right, but if'n I catch the critter who did this . . ." The magistrate peered into the back of the wagon at Jacob's master. "S'pose I ought'a tell yer master about him. He can keep an eye out. Yeh be goin' on yer rounds already, eh?"

"Yes, we be," Jacob answered trying not to panic. "But couldn't yeh tell me instead? He's had a long day and well, I don't ken waking him."

The magistrate chuckled. "I guess I could. Yer master's got a temper at the best of times; I spec he aint so friendly when he's woke." He rode a few steps closer, and stared at the master. "Be he well? Yeh sure he's not sick?"

Jacob glanced at the master over his shoulder. It was suspicious that he lay so quiet. *It's not going to work*, he worried. "I . . . I told yeh he had a hard day," he said.

The magistrate isn't going to buy it. What should I do?

But suddenly his master stirred, and then settled back, and began to softly snore. Jacob couldn't believe his eyes and ears, but he looked back at the magistrate who grinned, and said, "Yeh don't need to lie to me, Jacob. I know a drunken man when I see one." He wheeled his horse away, and said, "Yeh be sure and tell him about the attack when he wakes up though, all right?"

"I shall," Jacob assured him and, to his immense relief, the magistrate replaced his hat and, with a final nod, moved on.

Jacob clicked to Bobby to also continue. He didn't trust himself to look back until they had rounded the bend. The magistrate was gone.

The master was still snoring, but Jacob knew it had to be Mateo's doing. He leaned over, looked under the seat, and found the little imp grinning at him from the small space between the corpse and the wagon side.

"Yeh can stop snoring," he said, "and come out. He motioned for Mateo to come, and the boy squirmed out. "Yeh did good," Jacob told him, but the boy just gazed at him uncertainly.

What is the Spanish word for 'good'? Jacob knew he knew it. *Oh yes! 'Brain-o.'* He pointed at Mateo and said, "Yeh: brain-o."

The boy's face lit up. "Si? Bueno?" He jumped up from the baseboard, and threw his arms around Jacob. "Usted es bueno. Muy bueno."

Jacob could not remember the last time he had been hugged, and he hugged the boy back fiercely. "Yer me brother now, Mateo," he said. "It is yeh and me. I'm going to take care of yeh. I won't ever let anything happen to yeh." He knew the boy didn't understand a word he said, but he didn't care. He understood them, and he meant every one. He was going to take care of him.

And, in that moment Jacob became a man. He did not need a bar mitzvah ceremony. Accepting responsibility for Mateo's welfare had made him a man.

He pushed the boy gently back to the baseboard, and watched as he curled up and quickly fell asleep. The boy's faith in him was at once deeply satisfying and terrifying. Did Mateo not know the danger they both were in? Yet, as he stared down upon the imp, a confident peace grew within him until it spilled out in a huge grin.

He had a brother now; a boy to watch his back. Twice in one night Mateo had saved him. Together they would survive; Jacob knew they would.

He clicked to the horse, and drove on wondering what he should do. He knew that when morning came his master's family would miss them and the magistrate would be seeking him as well as the girl's attacker. A wave of nausea swept over him as he realized the magistrate now knew which way he had gone.

He considered maybe trying to turn the girl's misfortune to his advantage. Perhaps he could convince the magistrate that this same fugitive had attacked him and his master; in the scuffle his master had been killed.

But he very quickly discarded that idea. He did not believe he could convince the magistrate that his master had been killed by a pitchfork wielding fugitive on the King's Highway. It would be far more likely that, when the murder was discovered, he would be blamed for the girl's assault as well.

There was nothing he could do except make as much distance as he could before morning.

To add to his worries, the right rear wheel began to groan. He clenched his fist in frustration. That wheel had been giving them trouble for the past month, but his master had been too cheap to get it repaired properly. He had merely continued to order Jacob to fix it as best he could, and drive it. Jacob knew it was only a matter of time before it failed completely.

What was he going to do if it broke down in the middle of nowhere when he had to make miles? He would not be able to simply abandon the wagon with a corpse in it. But, since there was nothing he could do, he gritted his teeth and kept driving. He hoped it would not get so loud as to awaken people in the houses they passed.

The road eventually came to the ford across the river. Jacob saw it was quite deep, but urged Bobby into it. Everything was fine until they were half way across when he felt the wagon sway and lurch. The right rear wheel had fallen off. Faster than Jacob could react, the back of the wagon dropped, the water surged, and the wagon flipped. The horse screamed, and Jacob found himself thrown into the water. He came up gasping and looked frantically for Mateo only to find him bobbing like a cork and gamely swimming toward him.

Obviously the boy was a good swimmer; was that a smile on his face? Did nothing worry the imp? He was acting as if being awakened by a dunking was an everyday occurrence - almost as if he was enjoying it.

Jacob stared at him for a moment. Did the fact that he had killed a man a few hours hence not weigh upon Mateo's mind? How could it not? It made him wonder what other horrors the boy may have experienced in the past.

He heard Bobby scream again, and saw the poor horse flailing frantically. He quickly went to cut him loose. Then he looked for his master's corpse and saw an arm sticking out from under the wagon.

He had to get it out. He struggled to lift the wagon. Mateo joined him, but though they could lift it, they could not hold it up and pull the corpse out at the same time. But they simply had to.

"Jacob, be that yeh?"

Jacob jerked his head around. Mr. Sablonski stood silhouetted against the moon. Jacob would normally have been glad to see him, but under the circumstances was terrified; he could not allow him to see his master was dead. But before he could do anything, the man had splashed to him, and thrown the wagon over.

Hoisting the master to his back, Mr. Sablonski carried him to the bank, and laid him carefully down. Kneeling over him, he listened carefully for a breath, and then stared at Jacob. "Your master is dead!"

"I know," Jacob admitted. How could he explain? Could he make Mr. Sablonski believe him?

The man came over, and put his hand on Jacob's shoulder. "You must not blame yourself. You did everything you could."

Jacob struggled to understand, and stared at him fearfully.

"It was not your fault," Mr. Sablonski said. He glanced back at the corpse, and shook his head. "You could not get him free quickly enough. These things happen."

He believed his master had drowned! For a brief instant Jacob dared to hope everyone would believe it. But he was sure when the day came the wounds in his back would become plain and the truth would be known.

"We must load him into my wagon," said the tinker, "and take him to the tavern up the road. Grab his legs."

Jacob obeyed, but his mind was racing to find a way to escape. He could not think of a way. Mr. Sablonski lifted Mateo into the wagon, and climbed up himself. Jacob had no choice but to follow him.

"Who is the boy?" the man asked.

"What?" Jacob had been distracted. "Oh. He . . . he's . . ." He considered lying to his friend. Perhaps he could then get Mateo safely away. But he knew his master's wife and loathsome daughter would soon get the law on his trail; Mateo would be caught, and then things would be far worse for him. "My master purchased his labor earlier today."

Mr. Sablonski peered at the boy sympathetically. "That's a shame." He shook his head. "No boy should be sold like a slave."

His words gave Jacob a new hope. "Mr. Sablonski," he said tentatively, "could you . . ." Did he dare ask? "Would you leave Mateo and me here?"

His friend considered him.

Jacob plunged on quickly. "Tell them you couldn't find us. Everyone shall think we were drowned." He searched Mr. Sablonski's face; he couldn't tell what he was thinking. "Please. Let them think we are both dead."

The man pulled on his beard a few seconds, and glanced at Mateo. "Who knows what they'd do with you. What kind of master you'd end up with."

He regarded Jacob. "What would you do? Where'd you go?"

Jacob shrugged. "I don't know. Just run; get as far away as I could."

Mr. Sablonski pulled on his whiskers again. "You'd be seen. And even if you made it away, how would you live? You'd have to eat something - - live somewhere."

Jacob did not have an answer. He only knew he had to run.

Mr. Sablonski seemed to reach a decision. "Do you know the fork where the road veers to go north?" When Jacob nodded, he continued, "Go there and hide. I'll meet you there when I can." He eyed him sternly. "I may be a while. I've never hauled a corpse into town before; I don't know how long the magistrate shall detain me. But keep yourself concealed until I come, you hear?"

Jacob nodded. This offer of help was unexpected and almost made him collapse with relief. But it also motivated a terrible guilt, and for a moment Jacob considered refusing it. He knew the risk Mr. Sablonski was taking; aiding a servant's escape had dire consequences. And, although he did not know it, the man was not only offering to aid a servant's escape, but that of a murderer. Jacob felt he ought to at least tell Mr. Sablonski the truth, but he could not bring himself to do so.

"I know an Amish couple who need help on their farm," continued the tinker. "I think they'll give you room and board for your labor." He grinned at Jacob. "They'll work you hard, but you'll be a free man, able to stay, or go, as you choose. Would you find that agreeable?"

Jacob had to resist the urge to throw his arms around him in gratitude. "That would be . . . that would be very agreeable. Thank you."

Mr. Sablonski nodded. "You are welcome, Jacob. You remember I told you if you ever needed my help I would do all in my power to do so." He pointed his chin at the forest beside the road. "Go quickly, before anyone else comes."

14 Freedom

July, 1767

It wouldn't be safe to use the road, so Jacob led Mateo cross country to the fork, staying to the woods as much as possible. When they had to cross open fields he felt exposed, and expected to be stopped every moment. He kept telling himself it was too late at night, no one would be abroad, but the moon was so bright, he still worried. When he remembered the man who had attacked the Jamison gal it only added a new worry. What would he do if Mateo and he ran into him?

It seemed to take a long time to make it to the fork, and he started to worry Mr. Sablonski would get there before him. Surely he would wait, wouldn't he? Of course he would.

Yet, surely the man could not simply sit at the fork for long without attracting attention. If someone came by, how could he explain his idleness? He urged Mateo into a run.

When they arrived, Mr. Sablonski was not there. Had he already come and gone?

"No," Jacob told himself firmly. *He would never do that. I don't care if he did have to sit idle waiting for us; he would find an excuse to do it.*

He led Mateo into the bushes, and lay down. The boy dropped beside him. For the first time, the boy seemed scared. Jacob smiled at him, and held out an arm, and the boy snuggled against him and asked something; Jacob could not understand him.

He shook his head, and whispered, "sh-h-h." Mateo nodded, laid his head in a crook of his arm, and was soon snoring softly.

Jacob wished he could sleep; he was very weary, but he was far too worried.

What was happening in the village? Surely Mr. Sablonski had found the magistrate by then; had the magistrate noticed the holes in their master's back? Had Mr. Sablonski? What would they do if they had? Would Mr. Sablonski betray them?

He gazed down upon the boy. How could he sleep? He would have thought Mateo would be even more terrified than he; the boy could not even understand English, and he did not know Mr. Sablonski.

Mateo stirred, and tensed. But when he saw Jacob beside him, he smiled, pulled Jacob's arm tighter around himself, and promptly fell back asleep.

That is why he can sleep; he trusts me to protect him. The thought was comforting and terrifying at the same time. *How can he trust me, he doesn't even know me.* Yet he felt he knew Mateo very well indeed although they had met only scant hours earlier. He guessed Mateo felt the same way.

But should he trust me so? How can I protect him?

It seemed hours had gone by before he finally heard the tinker's wagon coming up the road. The familiar clatter sounded like the bells of heaven.

It came even with them, and stopped. He wanted to rush out, and hide in the wagon, but was suddenly afraid. Could he trust Mr. Sablonski? What if he had discovered the murder, and was trying to trap them?

The man was peering piercingly into the brush, and Jacob realized he had no choice but to trust him. He awoke Mateo, and the two of them hurried to the wagon, and climbed in. Without a word, Mr. Sablonski clicked to his horse, and they continued down the left fork of the road.

To Jacob's surprise, Mr. Sablonski then climbed back into the bed of the wagon also. Jacob glanced up at the seat to find he had tied the reins off.

"Aren't yeh going to drive?" he asked.

"No," the tinker said with a grin as he shifted a bundle to make a pillow. "I never drive at night; just tell ol' Barney there where I want to go. He knows the way better'n I do." He lay down, put his straw hat on his stomach, and patted the bed beside him. "Lay yerselves down. There's plenty of room for us all."

Mateo was soon asleep again, but Jacob's conscience was bothering him. He wasn't being fair to Mr. Sablonski, and he knew it. The man could end up in a great deal of trouble for aiding them. He had to know what he was doing.

Jacob did not allow himself to think about what Mr. Sablonski might choose to do then.

"Mr. Sablonski?"

"Yes?"

Jacob was glad; at least he was not yet asleep. "I have somewhat to tell you."

"Do you now?"

"Yes." He struggled how to go about telling him. How does one confess to a murder? How could he make his friend understand what had really happened? He heard the man clear his throat.

"You know," said Mr. Sablonski, "it was passin' odd." He sat up a bit and, leaning on one arm, regarded Jacob. "The magistrate and I happened to spot your master's horse in the road, and caught him. He had me accompany him to the mill with the horse and the corpse. We didn't want to have to transfer the corpse to another wagon, you see." He paused, and then continued sadly. "I sure did not look forward to informing the missus though. I was glad that task was the magistrate's. I didn't envy him it." He paused again, and then added quietly. "When we got to the mill, we put the horse in his stall."

Jacob froze. He tried to appear natural, but he didn't see how Mr. Sablonski could help noticing he was not. It felt like he was sweating from every pore on his body.

The blood on the floor! There had been blood on the floor; on the pitch fork too. Had Mr. Sablonski or the magistrate noticed it? It would have been dark in the barn; they might have missed it. Mighten they?

But Mr. Sablonski had said something had been odd. Jacob finally forced himself to ask, "What was passing odd?"

The man arched his eyebrows. "When we got there, we found the missus in the barn with a candle scrubbing the floor with lye."

Jacob sprang upright. She knew! She knew? But if she knew, why was she . . . ? She was erasing the evidence. She was trying to help him?

He glanced at Mr. Sablonski to find him staring at him keenly.

"Mr. Sablonski," he said again. "There is somewhat I must tell you."

The man squinted at him, pursed his lips, and pulled at his chin whiskers a moment. "I think it would be best if you didn't."

"But . . ."

He held up a hand. "I live in that village," he said. "If the magistrate was to ask me if I knew something about . . . well, about what happened tonight . . ." He looked Jacob in the eye. "I wouldn't be able to lie for you; not about . . ." He ran his fingers through his whiskers. "But I can't tell him what I don't know, now can I?"

"But," Jacob protested, "I have to . . . I can't allow you . . ."

Mr. Sablonski put a finger over Jacob's mouth. "I trust you, Jacob. Whatever you and your missus did, you did because you had to. That is all I need to know; all I ever desire to know." He took Jacob's shoulder in his hand. "And I told you years ago if you ever needed my help I'd do whatever I could. I meant it then, and I mean it still."

He lay back, and reached his hand into his pocket. "There is one thing more." He passed a folded parchment to Jacob. "Your missus set you free."

Jacob took the parchment dumbly. "She knows I'm not dead?"

"She does not know it; she hopes it. She dictated it to the magistrate, just in case you were not, and gave it to me to hold."

"She dictated it?"

"Your missus couldn't read nor write."

Jacob lay down, and allowed the truth to seep over him. He was free! The missus had set him free. A fear seized him, and he sprang back up.

"Mateo too? She set him free as well, did she not?"

"Aye. Mateo is also free." He passed a second parchment to him. "You'll keep it for him?"

Jacob sank back in relief. She had set Mateo free as well as himself. He was not sure what he would have done if she had not.

He wished it was light enough to read the parchment to make sure it was true, but the moon, which had been so bright earlier, was now screened in mists. He would have to wait until the morning. He carefully put the precious manuscripts deep into his pocket. He must not lose them.

He rolled on his side away from Mr. Sablonski. He didn't want him to see him cry yet he could not restrain the tears. "God bless the missus," he prayed. "God bless her."

He didn't know how long he wept and prayed, but he was awakened by the thud of the wagon fils against what he discovered was a barn.

Mr. Sablonski sat up beside him, and said, "We're here. That's how the ol' boy wakes me up; thuds the fils against the barn door." He climbed out of the wagon. "Come help me unharness him, and I'll get you settled in the loft. I reckon you can abide one more night, what's left of it, in a barn. I'll introduce you to the Gerbers in the morn."

Jacob was happy to comply. He didn't care if he had to sleep in a barn the rest of his life. He was free!

End of *Jacob's Bondage*

book one of *Jacob's Struggle*

Jacob's

Youth

Book two of:

Jacob's Struggle

CONTENTS

1   The Gerbers

September, 1767

Jacob squeezed the teat again. He could get nothing from it. He felt the bag and found it flaccid and empty. It had produced no milk at all? The two near teats had been fine. The far fore teat was full . . . but the far aft was empty. He again squeezed the fore teat and was rewarded with a healthy spurt.

What could be the matter with the aft teat?

How was he to tell Ezra? The loss of a fourth of a cow's production would be a hard blow for the Amishman to bear. And could the condition, whatever its cause, spread to the other three teats?

He did not look forward to telling him.

Then he heard the muffled snicker.

Mateo!

He peered under the cow behind him at the boy busily milking it. Had the snicker been his imagination? No! There it was again.

That little imp! Somehow he had snuck out and drained the teat; how Jacob did not know. He glanced into the boy's bucket. Sure enough, it was much fuller than his own.

He snuggled back against his cow, and began to drain the last teat. *Oh well, the joke is on him. I don't mind only doing three fourths of the job.* However, he found milking only one teat was much harder than milking two; it threw off his rhythm.

Yet thinking of Mateo made him feel happy all over. Jacob could hardly believe he had only known the boy a few short months.

So much had changed so fast, but Mateo was the best change of all; even better than gaining his freedom. Having a brother, even if he was an adopted brother, had made him realize how very much he had missed being part of a family. He was no longer alone.

And Mateo was smart. Jacob was amazed how many German words he already knew. Of course Jacob had picked up a healthy smattering of Portuguese trying to learn to communicate with Mateo. One of the first things he had learned was that Mateo was Portuguese; he emphatically did not want to be called a Spaniard.

The years Jacob had spent as an indentured servant to the brutal miller now seemed like a horrible nightmare from which he had finally awakened. And Mateo had been the one to free him. Jacob shuddered as he remembered the terrifying night he had been pinned under his master's immense bulk with a knife at his throat. His master had been going to kill him.

Thank God Mateo had killed him first. But then, of course, he and Mateo had been forced to flee. He had known no-one would believe they were innocent.

As he had many times before, Jacob thanked God for Mr. Sablonski who had come to their aid, and brought them to the Gerber's.

The Gerbers knew Mateo was not his real brother. Yet they were trying to keep the boys together. Still, Jacob worried they could ill afford to keep them both. Their farm was a frontier farm, not long hewn from the wilderness, and far from prosperous. And, while Ezra needed a hired hand since his children were girls and too young to boot, he did not need two. How long would it be before they were forced to suggest separating the boys?

And that Jacob was determined to not allow.

Still, what shall I do when that day comes?

He finished his cow, and carefully set the pail aside. He stood, stretched his back, and decided to forget his worries about the future.

"God provides what we need only when we need it," he remembered his father saying often. "We may wish it to be otherwise, but in this way He teaches us to trust."

I shall trust God to provide for us, he thought, but then he worried, *Does God recognize Mateo as my brother?* He felt He did but, to be sure, he stepped into a corner and pled, "God of Heaven and Earth; God of my ancestors, Abraham, Isaac, and Jacob, hear my prayer. May Mateo be my brother in Your eyes. Provide a way for us to remain together."

He heard Ezra come into the barn from tending the fowl. The Amishman kept chickens, turkeys, and pheasants in a coop beside the barn. They, along with venison, were the chief source of meat for their table. Fortunately for Jacob, he was too poor to raise swine.

For a moment, Jacob was embarrassed to be found praying, but his boss only nodded soberly, and said, "'Tis good to speak with the Lord in the morning," and climbed into the loft to throw some straw down for the cows' bedding.

Jacob was ashamed; he should have thrown the straw down so Ezra would not have to. He grabbed up a fork, and began to remove the old straw and manure from under his cow. Mateo had finished his own cow and did the same. By the time they had finished, Ezra had descended from the loft, and he helped them spread fresh straw to make a warm comfortable bed for each.

Jacob looked at him shamefaced. "I'm sorry. You'll not find me slacking again."

"Slacking?" the man asked. He leaned upon his fork, and considered Jacob. "Were I to choose twixt finding you throwing down straw, or praying in a corner, I'd choose the latter every time. I want you to remember that."

Jacob did not know what to say and so merely nodded and then, taking the pails of milk, followed his boss and brother in to eat.

The eastern sky was already turning gray; another hour and the sun would rise. The day promised to be an excellent one.

Martha welcomed them at the door with a, "Gracious, look at all the milk you boys have. Set it on the counter there, and hurry to wash your hands. Your breakfast is nearly ready." She whipped back to her stove, her skirts swishing to keep up.

Jacob liked to watch her work; she was so quick, often she would be turning one way while her skirts were yet turning the other. But he couldn't stand, and watch her; Mateo was nearly done at the basin, and he hurried to take his turn.

She always seems surprised at how much milk we have, as if Mateo and I were responsible for it. It was foolish, he knew, but it never failed to make him feel good. He hurried to seat himself on the bench beside his brother, and watched Martha and her three little girls load the table.

As usual, the contrast betwixt Ezra, who was thin and sober, and his wife and daughters, who were each round as a plum and happy as a fountain, was almost jarring. The four were talking and laughing so fast he wondered how any of them could listen to the others. Mateo leaned over, and whispered, "They sound like chickens."

Jacob snorted, and tried to pretend it was a cough. But it was hard not to continue laughing; the girls' laughter and talking did indeed sound a great deal like a flock of chickens cackling and squawking. But, far from annoying Jacob, he found it very enjoyable. After the solitude to which he was accustomed, it was like being wrapped in a warm soft quilt.

The table was soon loaded, and Jacob eyed the food with appreciation. *The Gerbers do know how to feed boys, even though they have only girls.*

2   A New Master?

May, 1768

Ezra was just finishing the chapter of scripture when Mateo jumped up, and cried, "Mr. Sablonski!"

It was their practice for Ezra to read aloud one chapter from the Bible each morning after the girls had cleared the breakfast away, and Jacob was just about to scold Mateo, thinking it was another of his pranks, when he heard the unmistakable rattle of the tinker's wagon.

Ezra gave them one of his rare smiles. "Yes, the tinker said he'd come this morning early. I wanted to surprise you boys."

Jacob did not answer, only grinned.

"Mama," the Amishman said, "bring what you held back from the table." Ezra and Martha always referred to each other as 'Papa' and 'Mama'. He turned to Jacob. "What say you and Matt fetch him in for a bite?"

Jacob jumped up, and hurried to the door, with Mateo running before him.

Mr. Sablonski was already tying off his horse. He turned just as Mateo threw his arms about him.

Jacob watched jealously wishing he was young enough to follow his example, but knowing that even if he was, he would not have done so. Even at that age he had been far too reserved to act so.

"Well, well," laughed Mr. Sablonski, disengaging himself from the boy, "What an exuberant welcome." He came to Jacob, and put one arm around him fondly. "How are you boys?"

Jacob drank in the embrace hungrily, looked up at him with a grin, and said, "Very well indeed, thank you." He grew serious. "Truly, we thank you. We shall never be able to repay you for your kindness. And the Gerbers are just wonderful to us."

"I knew they would be," Mr. Sablonski said, "and it was my pleasure to help you."

Mateo was dancing about them like the imp he was, but Mr. Sablonski ignored him, took both of Jacob's shoulders in his hands, and said, "It shall always be my pleasure. I would help you more if you'll take it."

Jacob nodded. "How?"

"Later." Mr. Sablonski took two quick steps, and pretended to try to catch Mateo who danced away laughing, only to run back and tackle him. Jacob watched intrigued as they wrestled together for a few moments. How did Mateo and Mr. Sablonski, who could hardly communicate, understand each other so perfectly?

Suddenly Mr. Sablonski leaned over, grabbed Mateo by one ankle, and slung him up-side-down over his shoulder.

"I know Ezra and Martha are waiting to feed me," he said. "They insist upon it every time I come, no matter what time of the day it is." He grinned at Jacob. "It would appear Martha is working her magic on you as well. Best take care, or she'll make you as plump as one of her own."

Jacob certainly hoped she would not. "Ezra is not plump."

Mr. Sablonski winked. "He works it off." He set Mateo upon his feet, led them into the house, and added, "But so shall you."

The snack Martha had provided, which would have fed thrice their number, was the most pleasant event Jacob could remember. Because of Mr. Sablonski's travels he knew a multitude of stories and was pleased to tell them, and for once Ezra and Martha did not seem to be in any hurry to begin their day's work.

But eventually it was over, and the men and boys went out to his wagon. Jacob was amazed to see him lift down eight large tin tubs. He glanced at Ezra. "You bought all of these?"

"No," Ezra said. "Mr. Sablonski is only loaning them to us. If things go as planned, when he returns we'll have them filled with honey."

Jacob remembered Ezra had told them he wanted them to find him a hive of bees. He already had two hives but he wanted a third. How they were to find a hive, Jacob had no idea, but Ezra had promised to teach them.

"That shall be your only task on the morrow," he had told them the night before, "and I am sure you shall enjoy it."

Jacob looked at the tubs in amazement. *Ezra hopes to fill all of them with honey?* It was hard to believe. He heard Mr. Sablonski say, "I would speak with Jacob privately if he shall." He looked up to see Ezra point his chin for him to follow the man who was already striding to the barn.

When they were in the barn Mr. Sablonski sat against one wall and indicated Jacob should join him.

"I'm going to talk to you man to man, Jacob. You are of an age when your father, had you one, would establish your future. You could, of course, remain a hired hand all your life, or perchance make an independent living as a farmer. But you don't strike me as a boy who could abide either of those. If you would escape those fates, you must act now."

"What do you mean?"

"You must learn a trade." The man examined a bit of dirt with great intensity before slowly adding, "And that shall entail apprenticing yourself to a tradesman."

"Apprenticing myself?" Jacob felt sick. Apprenticing was another word for indenturing. He had only just gained his freedom; was he now to relinquish it?

"Apprenticing is not the same as indenturing," Mr. Sablonski said. "Your master would be bound to teach you his trade, feed and house you well, and outfit you before you left him with all of the tools needed for you to establish yourself as an independent man."

"But he would still be my master."

"Yes," the man said soberly, "that he would. But you shall be free to choose your master and may negotiate the terms under which you shall serve before you accept him."

When Jacob did not reply, Mr. Sablonski said, "I have a friend, Mr. Wallace, who is a smith. I believe you would like him and enjoy serving him. Moreover I believe you would enjoy being a smith. You always seem to want to know how things work and how things are made. As a smith you shall."

The walls of the barn were closing in upon Jacob; he had to force himself to breathe.

Mr. Sablonski sighed. "I know this is hard for you. You know I would not suggest it if I did not believe it was for the best."

Jacob nodded.

The man continued relentlessly. "It is not only your future you must consider, it is your present. You must realize by now that one boy is all the Gerbers need, and that providing for both of you shall strain their resources."

Jacob nodded again, but buried his head in his arms. He had known the Gerbers could not keep them both, but hearing Mr. Sablonski say it had made him feel like an unwanted burden.

He felt his friend's hand stroking his back. "Now Jacob, you know I did not mean that the way it sounded. The Gerbers are very fond of you. Nonetheless, it is the simple truth; and a truth which must be faced." He waited until Jacob looked at him. "The present situation cannot be maintained for long. Either you act to change it, or circumstances shall force it to change."

He leaned closer to Jacob's face. "It is always preferable to choose to change one's situation before circumstances force a change, for you then have far more control over what your new situation shall be."

"So I must apprentice myself to the smith?" Jacob whispered.

"No, Jacob," answered the man. "I advise you do so, but you need not. It shall be your decision. And you ought not to decide today either for or against. I am giving you the advice; I would have you consider it. I shall return through here in three days. Perhaps you could give me an answer by then?"

Jacob knew Mr. Sablonski wanted him to agree; believed this was the best thing for him; likely had already approached the smith concerning it. Perhaps if Jacob rejected the apprenticeship it would embarrass Mr. Sablonski. He did not want to embarrass him; he wanted to please him.

But he could not bring himself to agree. And he could not promise to be able to give him an answer in three days. How could he?

He finally answered, "I shall try."

Mr. Sablonski clapped him upon the shoulder. "That is all I ask." He stood and helped Jacob to his feet. "I must go, I fear. I've many miles to cover before I sleep."

Jacob followed him numbly from the barn.

3   The Bees

May, 1768

Jacob stood with Mateo and Ezra and watched Mr. Sablonski clatter away until he disappeared around the bend. Then Ezra clapped both boys on their shoulders and asked, "You boys ready to find the wild hive?"

They both nodded, and Ezra held up a milk weed pod and pointed at it as he told Mateo to fetch him some more. Mateo raced around the barn to where milkweeds were plentiful, and Ezra strode to the wood pile, and picked up a chip half the size of his hand. "Jacob," he said, "Remember the pine tree we cut yesterday?"

Jacob nodded.

"Run there with this chip, and scrape up a generous supply of sap. Then meet Matt and me in the hay field, all right?"

Jacob caught the excitement of the usually staid man, and ran. The pine stump was covered with sap; he knew better than to get any on his fingers; pine sap was very sticky. But it was easy to scrape a large dollop onto the chip, and he then ran to the hay field. Ezra and Mateo were already awaiting him in the center of the field, and he hurried to join them. He wondered why they needed pine sap and milkweed pods to find a wild hive.

Ezra glanced at the dollop of sap. "That's finc, Jacob. Set it beside the pods yonder."

Jacob saw the pile of pods some feet away, and carefully set his chip beside them. The field was filled with wild flowers; the sun was shining so bright the colors could almost be felt, and the perfumes were intoxicating. There was just a hint of cold in the air, but the sun was warm. He was glad to be alive. Many bees were flitting from one blossom to another. He had to be careful not to step upon them.

When he had returned, Ezra asked, "You see all these bees? Some are from my hives, some from Levi's down the road, but some are from the wild hive. We are only interested in the wild bees."

"How can we tell which are which?"

"Ignore the bees flying about low," said Ezra. "Watch those flying high. Notice they always fly in a straight line to or from the field. That shall tell you which they are. My bees come from where I keep them in the orchard, Levi's come from yonder, but the wild come from the forest to the north. See, there is one now."

Jacob did see. He watched it settle to attend a blossom.

Ezra knelt behind the wild bee, and the boys copied him. "Watch closely now."

Jacob watched. The bee finished with the flower and rose, buzzed about a moment, and then settled upon a new flower. The trio followed it. Jacob still did not know what he was to see.

But then Mateo pointed at the bee, and cried, "He has bags on his legs!" and Jacob saw the bee did indeed have tiny bags attached to the sides of its legs which were slowly swelling as the bee filled them. He looked at Ezra in surprise. He had not known bees carried bags on their legs.

Ezra grinned. "You see them. Good. Watch until he fills them, and then you shall see him fly straight back to his hive."

Sure enough, after a few more blossoms, the bags were bulging, and the bee shot straight up in the air about eight feet, circled, and shot off like an arrow straight for the forest. Jacob tried to follow it with his eyes, but quickly lost it; there were too many other bees buzzing about.

"Find another wild bee," said Ezra, "and I'll show you how to track it."

They soon found one, and, while the boys kept watch of it, Ezra fetched a pod and the chip of sap. He broke the pod open to expose the fluffy seeds within, and, taking several seeds, dipped them in the sap being careful to get neither his fingers nor the fluff in the sap. Then, in a quick motion, he stuck them onto the rear of the bee. The bee was almost finished filling his bags, and soon rose and circled for his return to his hive. Jacob saw it flew much slower than had the first bee; the fluff on its rear slowed it considerably. It also made it very easy for him to see as it buzzed away.

"Run after it," yelled Ezra. "Follow it as long as you can."

Both boys were happy to obey. They followed it quite some distance into the trees before they finally lost sight of it. Jacob had seen that it flew perfectly straight except when it was forced to detour around a tree. But after a detour it always returned to a straight flight. He led Mateo back to Ezra. He was surprised how far they had come.

"Take note of the direction the bee was flying," said Ezra. "The hive lies somewhere in that direction." He handed the chip of sap to Jacob, gave three seed pods to Mateo, and pointed at Levi's hay field. "You'll find bees in his field as well. Go to the far side of his field and tag and follow another wild bee. If the hive is close you'll find his flight shall be at an angle to your first bee. The hive shall be at the intersection of the two lines. But likely the hive is further away than that which shall necessitate you going further abroad. Keep going until the flights begin to angle. Then travel at a ninety degree angle until you find bees that fly at an angle which is ninety degrees from our first bee. It shall then be a simple matter to walk straight into the woods on that line until it intersects this line. There you should be able to locate their hive. When you do, come and get me. Do you understand all of that?"

When Jacob nodded, Ezra clapped him on the back. "Good boy." He started back to the barn, but turned to say, "Oh, and Jacob?" When Jacob looked at him, he finished, "Enjoy yourselves."

Jacob grinned back at him; he was sure they would.

It took the boys most of the rest of the day to locate the hive. It was at least three miles inside the forest. Neither boy tired of the task, and often would chase a bee much further than was necessary to determine its flight. Jacob was pleased to find he had very sharp eyesight; he could often spot a bee before Mateo did and follow it longer.

He was almost disappointed when they found the hive, but when he saw how many bees were leaving and entering it he knew it was a very large hive, and grew excited. He led Mateo on a lively run back to the Gerber farm.

Ezra must have seen them coming for he met them halfway across the pasture. He seemed almost as excited as the boys were. "Did you find it?"

"Aye," Jacob crowed before he remembered to talk in German. "It's a big one."

"Huge!" Mateo said.

Jacob and Ezra both stared at him. Jacob wondered how he knew that word, but then remembered he had used it when they had found the hive. The little imp had remembered.

"It is huge," he assured Ezra.

"Huge enough to require all of Mr. Sablonski's tubs?" Ezra's eyes were sparkling; he was teasing them.

"Yes," Jacob answered pertly, "it is."

Ezra suddenly pursed his lips, and smacked his forehead. "Ach," he cried, "I forgot to give you a hatchet." He looked at the boys dismayed. "You needed to mark the tree and the path to it." He glanced at the sun. "We'll never locate it again in time." He shook his head. "Ah well, we've only lost a day. We'll relocate it in the morning, and then capture the bees tomorrow evening." He glanced at the boys. "It's not your fault, it is mine. But we can only capture the bees in the evening when they have settled."

"We still have time," Jacob protested. "We can lead you straight to the tree, I'm sure we can."

Ezra looked skeptical. "Even though you did not mark it?" He shook his head. "I don't know . . . you'll find all the trees look alike."

"No they won't. I know right where it is. Let me show you."

Ezra still looked unconvinced, but said, "Wait here for a moment while I fetch my things," and he hurried back to the barn. When he returned, he was carrying a new hive box, a tiny grass basket with a small drawstring, a hatchet, and the strangest utensil Jacob had ever seen. It looked like a little teapot with two very long slender spouts each of which was issuing a thin stream of smoke.

"All right," Ezra said, handing the hive box to Jacob for him and Mateo to carry, "Lead me to the hive."

With ease, Jacob led him straight to the tree, and pointed out the hole the bees were buzzing about.

Ezra looked at him astonished. "I didn't think you could do it," he admitted. "You must have an excellent sense of direction." He looked at the bees still flying to and fro. "It's still a bit early. We need for them to stop flying. While we wait, you boys could gather me some moss, damp bark, and grass, if you would."

The boys soon had small piles of each and Ezra opened the kettle and put a bit of each upon the coals already glowing there.

Jacob wondered what the odd utensil was for, but waited and watched. He saw the bees had almost stopped flying.

"It's time I start climbing, I guess," Ezra said, and, taking only the kettle and the tiny basket, he scaled the tree to the hole. "You boys stay there."

Jacob was surprised how agile he was. He was also surprised he showed no fear of the bees still buzzing about. "Aren't you worried you'll be stung?" he called.

"Ach," Ezra replied placidly, "you can't allow a few stings to deter you if you want to capture a hive."

How is he going to capture all those bees?

He watched as Ezra put one of the kettle's spouts into his mouth and saw that when he blew into his spout, a thick cloud of smoke spewed from the other.

Ezra aimed the second spout at the hole and blew smoke into the hive. Bees soon began to pour from the hole, but surprisingly, did not seem angry; they only crawled out upon the tree. Soon the tree all around the hole was covered by bees but Ezra kept blowing smoke. The smoke began to dwindle, and still the bees flowed forth.

Ezra pulled the spout from his mouth, and called down. "You are right, this hive is huge. Throw me up some more moss."

Jacob did so, but asked, "How many bees do you want? Isn't this enough?"

Ezra laughed, and answered, "I'm only after one bee, and she hasn't come out yet." He returned the spout to his mouth, and resumed blowing. Soon not only was the tree near the hole covered with bees, but Ezra's arms, legs, and back also.

"Ah ha," he finally crowed. "There she is." He dropped the pipe to the ground, carefully trapped a bee within his tiny basket, tied it shut, and began to descend.

Jacob picked up the pipe, and watched him. To his consternation he saw all the bees were following Ezra.

"Open the hive box," Ezra called as he dropped the last few feet.

Jacob hurried to obey, but when he had gotten it open, and he turned to Ezra, he fled in terror. Ezra was standing with a huge ball of bees which had swallowed the hand and much of the arm holding the basket.

Ezra laughed at him, and calmly lowered the ball into the hive box, and brushed the bees from his arm as if they were dust. Most of the bees dropped into the box, and remained there, the few which were flying about quite quickly joined them, and Ezra replaced the lid.

Jacob and Mateo stood watching him with slack jaws. "How did you do that?" Jacob finally managed to ask.

"Ach, it was easy," Ezra said. "The bee I captured in the basket was the queen bee. Once I had her, I controlled all the rest. Wherever the queen goes, the rest shall follow. They'll soon chew through the basket and free her, but by then they'll have accepted this box as their new hive. We'll give them a bit of their honey comb to keep them happy and healthy tomorrow."

"But how did you keep them from stinging you?"

"The smoke calms them. Bees communicate with smells; when they cannot smell, they are disoriented. Also, a bee shall not attack what it does not fear; if you stay calm, so shall it." He shrugged. "So long as you do not fear being stung, you shall not be." He smiled. "At least not much." He saw the kettle in Jacob's hand. "Ah good, you got the smoker. Give it to Matt. I'll need you to help me carry the hive."

Jacob obeyed, but did not like carrying his end of the hive; the bees were buzzing very loud and, despite what Ezra had said, he was afraid. The hive was heavy too. But they managed to transport it back to the farm's orchard to the stump Ezra had planned for it without incident.

Ezra positioned it carefully. "I'd step well back were I you," he warned.

Jacob did not need to be told twice; he backed well away from the hive, and made sure Mateo did also.

Ezra pulled the rag he had stuffed into the hole drilled into the side of the box, and ran to join them.

A cloud of bees poured out of the hole. They sounded very angry.

"Aren't you afraid they'll fly away?" Jacob asked.

"No," Ezra said. "The queen can no longer fly." He winked. "She used to, when she was younger, but no more. And since she shall stay, so shall the rest."

He put one arm around each boy. "You boys did well. Let's go for a bit of bread before we do the evening chores. I expect you're hungry."

Jacob realized he was hungry; more than hungry, famished. They had not eaten since breakfast. But could it really be time for evening chores? He glanced at the sun and saw it was. The day had flown by.

* * * *

That night snuggled against his brother, he thought back over the day. Ezra had been right; they had very much enjoyed searching for the hive. On the morrow they would cut the tree down and obtain the honey.

The part Jacob had enjoyed the most had been walking freely in the forest. He felt like he could have walked through the forest forever and never gotten tired. Part of him wished he had been able to.

But the quiet snores of Mateo and the three little girls made Jacob glad he was just where he was: in the bed he shared with his brother and under a thick warm quilt. After sleeping in straw in a barn for so many years, sleeping in a bed with a quilt was like heaven. It was true they had to share the loft of the house with the girls, but that he did not mind.

I can hardly believe how fortunate we are. The Gerbers, although we are only hired hands, treat us like family.

But he then remembered his conversation with Mr. Sablonski and his spirits fell. Why had Mr. Sablonski had to ruin an otherwise glorious day?

And what was he, Jacob, going to do? Mr. Sablonski was going to return in two days. He would expect an answer. Jacob knew he would want him to agree to apprentice himself to the smith.

But I don't want to!

Yet if he didn't, what would he do? Mr. Sablonski had been right; he would have to do something. And Mr. Sablonski thought becoming an apprentice was the right thing to do.

But I don't want to!

He wished he really could just walk into the forest forever; leave all his troubles behind.

Yet wishing changed nothing. He felt trapped. He had no choice; he was going to be bound again.

Still, Mr. Sablonski had assured him it would be his choice. He had said he would abide by his decision even though it was plain he wanted Jacob to apprentice himself to the smith.

I do not have to bind myself.

He was glad. It was settled. He would not be bound; he did not care what the future consequences might be.

Then, as if he were in the loft with him, he heard his father repeat something he had once told him: "It is a man's duty to do whatever is best for his family even if it means sacrificing himself."

It had been years since he had heard his father's voice even in his memory but he knew it. He even remembered the exact day and situation his father had said it.

He listened to the quiet snoring of the boy sleeping beside him.

Mateo is my family; the only family I have. I promised I would take care of him; he is depending upon me. What would be best for him?

He knew the answer; it would be best for Mateo if Jacob apprenticed himself. If he stayed, the Gerbers would be almost certain to be forced to conclude they were unable to keep both boys. They would prefer to keep him as the older of the two. Mateo would have to live with, and work for, someone else. Who knew how that new family might treat him? With the Gerbers, Mateo was happy, well cared for, and loved.

With Jacob gone, the Gerbers would be certain to keep him.

The decision was now obvious. When Mr. Sablonski returned he would tell him he would apprentice himself. He would do anything for Mateo; even bind himself to a new master.

4   The New Master

May, 1768

When Mr. Sablonski returned he found the eight tubs were indeed awaiting him filled with honey. He assured Ezra they would fetch an excellent price in Philadelphia.

Jacob and Mateo had both been introduced to the pleasure of honeycomb chewing. Any time they wished they could pull off a wad from the mound of screened wax and pop it into their mouth. At first it would be full of sweet honey, but would soon be only a wad of wax which would squeak against their teeth. They could chew it for as long as they chose; it would never decrease, and it was fun.

But of course they would spit it out after a bit to make room for a fresh wad; they only had to be careful not to allow Martha or her girls see them spit it out; she had declared she did not want disgusting wads of wax all over her yard. But Ezra had told them not to worry; the bees would clean up any wads. And indeed they did. Any wad they spat out disappeared within a very few hours.

They did not have to worry too much about Martha seeing them however, for she was exceedingly busy making candles. One shelf was already filled with dozens of the sweet smelling tapers.

Jacob was glad; he liked beeswax candles. Not only did they burn with a bright clear light, they always filled the room with their wild sweet odor.

Mr. Sablonski called him aside. "Have yeh considered my proposal?" he asked in English.

Jacob stared at the ground. "Aye." He forced himself to look him in the eye. "I'll apprentice myself as yeh advised."

His friend nodded. "Good." He put a hand on Jacob's shoulder. "I truly think yeh shall not regret it."

"Aye." Jacob replied. He hoped Mr. Sablonski was right. At the moment it felt like a catastrophe. "How long shall it be?"

"Let us walk as we talk, shall we?" suggested his friend. They walked, and he said, "Mr. Wallace, the smith, is asking for five years. I doubt me he'd settle for much less, although yeh would be free to negotiate for less."

"Negotiate?"

"Aye. I told yeh, yeh shall be free to negotiate the terms of yer apprenticeship. Yeh must both be satisfied with the terms before yeh agree." He stopped, and took Jacob's shoulder. "And if yeh are unable to agree on suitable terms, then he shall not accept yeh, nor shall yeh bind yerself. Do yeh understand?"

"Aye," Jacob said. What terms could ever make a five year bondage palatable? But he forced himself to smile at Mr. Sablonski and ask, "When shall we negotiate?"

"This afternoon, if yeh desire. I can drive yeh there on my way back to Philly."

Jacob did not desire it; he wished he could postpone it for a very long time, but he agreed.

* * * *

Mr. Sablonski pulled up before a long sturdy building, and tied his horse at the rail. It was not unpleasant, situated as it was in a small yard surrounded by oaks and maples, but it reminded Jacob of a warehouse.

"The smithy is in the rear," his friend said. "I'll take you around and introduce you to Mr. Wallace in a moment. But before I do, there is something I must address with you."

Jacob waited, but Mr. Sablonski was silent for several moments as if he were uncertain what he wanted to say. Finally he turned, and looked Jacob in the eye. "When you had first gained your freedom, and I brought you to the Gerbers, I sought only to provide for your needs to be met, and to allow you and Mateo to make a new start without the prejudice which sometimes follows former servants. Since your missus had set you free, I thought you had little to fear from discovery by those in Wynnewood. The magistrate had ruled your old master's death an accident. No one then doubted his verdict.

"Unfortunately that is no longer true. Miranda is convinced her father was murdered and, despite a complete lack of proof, is determined to convince others of it. She is succeeding far beyond my expectations; public opinion has gradually turned against you."

He paused for several moments, and then concluded, "It would no longer be safe for you to be discovered by anyone who knew your former existence. I fear you must take steps to prevent such a discovery. You must never go near Wynnewood; or Philadelphia, for that matter. What is more, I would suggest you change your name; you and Mateo both. Far too many people already know you as Jacob to change that, but I'd have you adopt a new surname and, from now on, Mateo must be referred to as Matt."

"What surname? Gerber? But most people know I am not a Gerber."

"No. Not Gerber. I have been thinking about this, and I would suggest 'Schram'. It is a good German name and so will cause you to blend in well in Berks County but, insofar as I know, there are no Schrams living here to question your relationship."

Schram, Jacob thought, *Jacob Schram*. He decided he liked it. He looked up at Mr. Sablonski, and nodded.

Mr. Sablonski smiled a sad smile. "So be it. I shall introduce you as such to Mr. Wallace." He put an arm around Jacob, and hugged him. "I am truly sorry you must take such a measure. I hope I can soon report that public opinion has turned against Miranda and her accusations and that you no longer must hide your identity."

Jacob nodded. He did not know what to say.

"Are you ready to meet Mr. Wallace?"

Jacob nodded. He was afraid to speak for fear his voice would betray him.

Mr. Sablonski peered at him, and put a hand gently upon his shoulder. "You still do not need to go through with it," he said. "You are here to negotiate terms. If, when you are done you are not completely satisfied with them, you are free to refuse him. You know that, do you not?"

Jacob again nodded. He didn't tell him he was determined to apprentice himself regardless of the terms.

"Very good. I'll take you round back to him. But then I'll be on my way. I fear you'll need to walk back to the Gerbers." Mr. Sablonski turned, and led Jacob around the building.

Jacob's first glimpse of his new master was reassuring. The smith was a large man with long brown hair which he had tied at the nape of his neck, muscles like an ox, and skin like old leather, but an open honest face which positively beamed at their appearance.

"Wheel now," he almost roared as he came toward them, "Be yeh the Jacob Am'm ta have the pleasure o' meetin'?"

His welcome and pleasure were so genuine Jacob found himself smiling back. His speech reminded him of one of his old master's clients. That particular client had been one of his favorites.

He extended his hand, which was enveloped in the smith's. "Jacob Ah be. A pleasure it is ta meet yeh as wheel."

The smith's eyebrows went up, and he grinned at Mr. Sablonski. "Yeh dinna tell me the lad could speak so grand."

Jacob liked how the 'r' in 'grand' rolled off the man's tongue and mentally rehearsed it.

Mr. Sablonski laughed. "I did not know." He looked at Jacob affectionately. "He is a boy who regularly surprises me." He put his hand on Jacob's shoulder and said in German, "I must be on my way. You'll be all right?"

Jacob glanced at the smith, and nodded. "I'll be fine. Thank you very much for the introduction. I'll do my best to not fail you."

"It was my pleasure, Jacob." He looked like he wanted to say more, but turned upon his heel and left.

The smith and Jacob considered each other for a long moment, and then the smith pointed to a large bellows attached to a forge, and said, "Ah'll be thankin' yeh to pump a roarin' hot fire, if yeh please."

Jacob was surprised. He had thought he was there to negotiate terms, not to be put to work, but the smith had asked so politely he went and began to pump. It was not hard labor, but after a bit began to be tiring. He was glad when Mr. Wallace told him he could quit for a spell as he grabbed an iron bar and thrust it into the inferno Jacob had created.

Jacob came around to where he could watch him.

The smith was holding the end of the bar with a large pair of tongs and slowly rotating it but grunted, "Take up the hammer yeh see upon the bench yonder."

Jacob hurried to obey. By the time he returned to the forge the end of the bar was glowing a bright yellow and Mr. Wallace yanked it from the fire, swung it to an anvil, grabbed up another hammer, ordered, "Hit th' bar exactly where Ah hit it as hard or soft as Ah do," and delivered the bar a mighty blow.

Jacob did his best to match the blow to the exact same spot. He hoped the smith would find it acceptable, but he had no opportunity to discover if he did for hardly had his hammer cleared the bar before the smith's was descending for another in a slightly different location.

BANG. . BANG. Bang . . bang. Thud . . thud. Tap-ity-tap . . tap-ity-tap. Thud . . Thud. BANG . . BANG. On and on the blows fell, sometimes hard, sometimes soft, sometimes in one spot, sometimes another until the bar was beaten down flat and cold. It was thrust back into the fire, and Jacob was ordered to pump the fire up again.

He wondered what they were making; he had tried hard to discern the rhythm and logic of their blows but had been unable to do so.

The metal was thrown back upon the anvil and the beating resumed, but to Jacob's surprise, they beat it into a completely new shape. He could see no resemblance to the first shape.

Over and over the procedure was repeated, heat the iron, beat it into a new shape, and then heat it up to beat it into another.

Finally Mr. Wallace stopped, and threw the misshapen clod of iron into a pan of water where it caused a volcano of steam to gush forth. The two of them stood staring at it for a moment.

"What did we make?" Jacob finally ventured to ask.

"Make?" grunted the smith considering Jacob with respect. "The only thing Ah intended to make was to make yeh tired; Ah wanted ta see how long yeh could last."

"I be not tired," Jacob lied. In truth he was nigh exhausted; the hammer felt like it weighed twenty pounds though he knew it was more like three.

"Aye," the smith gasped. "But Ah be. Come on," and he led the way into the building. "Ah've a barrel o' beer just inside th' door. Nothin'll light a man's fire again like a sip er two." He drew two large steins, and handed one to Jacob.

Jacob didn't tell him he had never drunk beer before, just carefully sipped it.

"Ach nae," cried the smith. "Yeh canna sip it like tha'. Beer yeh must quaff," and he drained his stein in one long drink.

Jacob did his best to match his example, and the steins were refilled and again drained. He began to feel slightly unsteady and bloated.

Fortunately the smith abandoned the barrel, settled himself upon a bench by the table, tore a hunk off a loaf of bread, and offered the loaf to Jacob.

Jacob took the bread, tore off a hunk, and seated himself upon the other bench.

"What do yeh ken?" asked the smith. "Shall yeh take ta smithin'?"

Jacob considered the question. They had not yet negotiated terms. Was this the beginning? Did this mean the smith was accepting him? "Aye," he finally answered. "I could smith."

"But would it pleasure yeh?" The smith eyed him critically. "Take a trade yeh do nae enjoy and yeh'll soon grow to despise it. Yeh may prosper with it, yeh mayhap grow rich, but yer days'll be long and dreary." He took a bite of his bread, chewed, and swallowed it before continuing, "A smith can prosper most anywhere he goes; yeh'll find few who are poor." He leaned across the table, and glared in Jacob's eye. "But no amount o' money can compensate fer long weary hours at a task yeh despise." He leaned back and said, "So Ah'll ask yeh again, 'Shall yeh take to smithin'?'"

"I . . . I don't know." Jacob swallowed. "I think I shall. How can I know?"

The corner of the smith's mouth twitched. "Yeh canna. If yeh'd answered yeh were sure yeh should, Ah'd o' sent yeh packin'. Th' only way yeh'll know is if yeh try it. And the only way Ah can tell if yeh've got what it takes is to try yeh."

He held out his hand. "Ah'll give yeh a trial o' a month. Come then Ah'll know what yeh're made of and if I care ta continue with yeh, and yeh'll either love smithin' or hate it."

Jacob stared at his hand, and swallowed. "There is somewhat I'd negotiate first."

The hand was withdrawn. "'Ey? Negotiate yeh say?" The smith considered him, but then grinned and, returning to the barrel, drew another two steins of beer." He settled himself to his bench, and plunked one stein before Jacob. "Gotta have my beer iffn we're to negotiate." Jacob was relieved to see he only took a small gulp. "Now, then. What be yer conditions?"

"I am a Jew," Jacob said carefully. "Thus I shall not work on the Sabbath; yer Saturday. I shall however be happy to do whatever yeh desire on Sunday." When he was in bondage formerly he had been unable to keep the holy days, but since he had been little more than a slave, it had not been his fault, and he had incurred no guilt. However, if he did not now negotiate the right to observe them, it would be his fault.

"Yeh'll do no work at my bidding upon a Sunday," growled Mr. Wallace, "That be my Sabbath." He sat for a moment considering. "But yeh'd be free to do whatever work yeh'd have a mind ta do for yerself upon a Sunday. Ah'd not forbid yeh." He scratched his chin. "As to workin' upon Saturday, Ah only smith Monday to Friday any rate. Saturday Ah tend my fields, such as they be. Ah'll not require yer aid fer that." He looked at Jacob. "Be there more?"

Jacob nodded. "There are five holy days in the year I'd also ask to be free."

"Be there more?"

"No."

"Yer terms are agreed ta." The hand was again extended.

Jacob reached to shake it, but pulled back at the last moment. "Since yeh said I could do as I chose on Sunday," he ventured tentatively, "I would ask leave to return to the Gerbers every Sunday for a visit." When the smith's eyebrows arched, he rushed to add, "I have a brother there yeh see." He stared hard at the table. "I'm gonna miss him . . . somethin' fierce." When the smith did not reply, he looked up to find him stroking his chin.

"Yeh 'ave reservations." When Jacob did not reply, Mr. Wallace continued, "Yeh must know, Jacob, Ah've 'ad my own reservations about takin' an apprentice."

Jacob's heart fell. "Yeh did?"

"Aye." The smith waved his hand about himself at the room. "Look't this room. Taint hardly space fer me let alone yeh. T'was always cramped and, when my missus died, Ah took to storin' things in it. Ah've been right worried how ta supply yeh space." He scratched his cheek. "And if the truth be told, Ah've become mighty attached to my solitude of a night. T'was nae sure Ah wanted ta give it up; yeh know?"

Jacob nodded soberly. It was over then; the smith didn't want him.

But Mr. Wallace continued, "Ah 'ad an idea just now which may salve both o' our reservations." He arched one eyebrow, and looked Jacob in the eye. "Do yeh think the Gerbers'd be willin' to give yeh board and room if Ah was to pay em?"

"Pay em?" Jacob asked. He was suddenly excited. "Aye. I'm sure they would. And their farm is only a forty minute walk from yer smithy."

"Aye," agreed the smith, "lessen that were yeh to obtain a horse." He cocked an eye at Jacob. "But come winter, it'd be a mighty cold walk. Are yeh sure yeh'd be willin'?"

"Oh yes!" To be able to board with the Gerbers with Mateo was worth any number of cold walks.

Mr. Wallace nodded. "Wheel then, both o' our reservations are eased. Yeh'll 'ave ever' night and the weekends w' yer brother, and Ah'll keep my storage and solitude." He cocked an eyebrow at Jacob. "But Ah'll be holdin' yeh to it." When Jacob nodded, the smith crossed his arms, considered for a moment, and then said, "Yeh offer the Gerbers three shillings a week. Iffn they balk, yeh kin give em four." He frowned. "No more'n four though. Ah could board yeh elsewhere for tha'."

Jacob held out his hand. "Agreed."

His hand was enveloped and shook. "Ah'll be expectin' yeh at dawn Monday then."

"Aye." Jacob stood, and began to the door. "Monday at dawn."

"Jacob," the smith called. When Jacob turned, he winked, and said, "Ah was right. T'was a real pleasure meetin' yeh."

Jacob nodded, and answered. "Aye. T'was a pleasure fer me as well." When the smith nodded, he turned again to go, but was again called back.

"Yeh will nae leave yer bit o' beer standin'?"

He laughed, returned to the table to drain the stein, and, on an impulse, clapped his new master on the shoulder. "Ah am lookin' forward to Monday."

"Aye," the man said. "We'll make the sparks fly, that we shall. Be off with yeh."

Jacob left. *It is true; I do look forward to working for Mr. Wallace. I hope he shall keep me on after the month.* For a moment he felt a pang of worry, but quickly shoved it aside. Surely he would prove himself worthy. Suddenly the five years to which he would be committing himself did not seem so long.

He stopped in mid stride. *Stupid, stupid, stupid,* he thought. *Does not Mr. Sablonski know every tradesman in the county? And did he not recommend Mr. Wallace, and say I would enjoy serving him?*

The terrible stress of the past few days had been horrible. *And it was all for nothing. I should have trusted him.*

Then he realized even Mr. Sablonski had not been able to arrange for him to remain with Mateo; that had been a fortuitous turn of events no one could have foreseen; none but God, and he remembered his prayer.

His heart welled with gratitude and he dropped to his knees, and thanked Him.

In the future, he resolved, *I shall trust my God and the friends He has given me and spare myself the un-necessary distress.*

5 Hannah

November, 1768

The weather was turning colder and Jacob walked briskly to keep warm. He loved these autumn mornings though; they made him feel so alive. The daily walk to and from the smithy, far from a burden, had become a favorite part of his day; he enjoyed his solitude. If only he had not the nagging worry things could not continue as they were.

Mr. Wallace seemed very pleased with him, but how long would he continue to pay three and a half shillings a week for his room and board if there was no work. That had been the fee agreed upon; the Gerbers would, Jacob was sure, have accepted three, mayhap less, but he had offered them three and a half. He had convinced himself they needed it and that the smith could afford it. Now he was starting to feel guilty and wished he had not for the steady stream of work from the surrounding farmers was rapidly dwindling. Would there be work enough through the winter for the smith to keep him on?

Yet when he arrived, Mr. Wallace announced it was time to move the smithy inside. Jacob was surprised; he had not known there was an inside. He had thought the entire building, except the room the smith used for his living quarters, had been used for storage.

Mr. Wallace opened a door, and showed him a sizable hall which contained a forge nearly as large as the one outside. "Everything else," he said, "the bellows, the several anvils, the large sharpening stone, and the myriad tools and shelves, all must be moved from the outside."

"But before we do so," Mr. Wallace's eyes gleamed, and he led Jacob to a cabinet, opened it, and showed him a rack containing seven gleaming new guns. Jacob gazed at them in amazement, and then at his master.

"Yeh're seein' my passion and joy," the man said. "Summers Ah make implements; they be good implements and Ah take pride in them, but they be heavy and ugly. But winters Ah make these." He took down one of the weapons, and caressed its smooth barrel. "It requires well forged steel and a steady hand to create a fine weapon. But the result is worth it. A gun is both a useful tool and a pleasure to behold. Each one is different with a personality o' its own." He handed it to Jacob. "Try it out."

Jacob ran his hand over the smooth wood, and inspected it. He had never seen a gun at close range before let alone held one. He gazed at the tiny parts of the flint lock on the side, and marveled at its intricate workmanship.

"Yeh ever fire a gun, Jacob?"

He tore his gaze from the weapon. "No," he admitted, "I never have."

"Wheel then," cried his master, "It be past time yeh did. What say yeh we do some shootin' next Sunday afternoon? Ah do nae think the Lord minds a bit o' shootin' on His day."

Jacob powerfully wanted to accept his invitation, but reminded his master Sunday was his day with Mateo. He knew the boy anticipated the day as much as he did. He did not want to disappoint him.

"Bring 'im along," the smith said. "Ah've been achin' to meet yer brother."

"Yeh mean it?"

"Aye. How old be he?"

How old is Mateo? Jacob did not know. "Nine," he finally said.

"Ach, plenty old enough to shoot. Ah spend the morning in church; would three o' the afternoon suit yeh. That'd give us a couple o' hours before dark."

Jacob could hardly believe his fortune. "Three would suit us fine."

"Good laddie," said his master. He took the gun, returned it to its rack, and closed the cabinet. "Let's move the smithy inside."

* * * *

It had taken most of the morning to move the anvils, the bellows, and the sharpening stone. They had then taken a lunch break.

There came a knock upon the door, and it opened to admit a barefoot girl with long braided brown hair and clear grey eyes.

"Me pa sent me to have yeh make him a new adz," she announced.

"I can move the remaining things whilst yeh make her adz," Jacob told his master.

"Nae," said the smith. "I'll move em. Ah am rather partial concerning my shelves and tools. Yeh make her adz."

"Me?"

"Aye. Yeh've helped me make several in the past weeks. Yeh know 'ow." He glanced at the girl. "Yeh'll pump the bellows for him will yeh, Hannah?" When she nodded, he said, "That's a lass," hove himself from the table, and disappeared out the door leaving Jacob and the girl to stare at each other.

Jacob said with a confidence he did not feel, "We may as well begin. I'm finished with my meal." He gulped down the last of the beer his master had set before him, and led her around to the inside smithy.

"Ach." He had no tools. "I must fetch the tools." He threw a shovelful of coal upon the fire which was already burning in the forge. "Pump up the fire, if yeh would, whilst I fetch them." He hurried from the room. He found her calm appraising grey eyes disconcerting.

Outside he collected the tools he needed, but asked Mr. Wallace if he was sure he wanted him to attempt making the adz.

"Nae," the smith said, thrusting a bar of iron into his hand, "I do nae want yeh to attempt it. Ah want yeh to do it. Go."

Jacob went.

He found Hannah had already built the fire into an inferno. He was impressed, but tried to act professional as he laid out his hammers and the plugs he would use to form the shaft hole. He thrust the end of the bar into the fire. "Yeh can back off the pace of yer pumping," he said. "I know it gets tiresome. Just pump it enough to maintain the fire."

She reduced her pace, but kept pumping.

Jacob concentrated upon his bar. He waited until a good foot and a half was glowing brightly and heated completely through. Then he pulled it out, swung it to the large anvil and, with a large chisel, cut off a foot. He thrust the remainder of the bar into the pan of water. He enjoyed the volcano of steam the hot bar produced. He thought it made him look and sound like he knew what he was doing, and it gave him confidence.

But he knew he only had a minute or so to shape the iron he had cut off, so he grabbed it with a pair of tongs, and began to beat it into shape. An adz needed a four inch sharp edge on a blade which tapered to two inches where it terminated in a shaft perpendicular to the edge, but the blade must also curve upward thirty degrees. He beat the edge first and then worked on the curve and the taper. He worked hard to make both the curve and taper uniform. He had to reheat it thrice before he was satisfied. He was aware of Mr. Wallace coming and going and watching him, but the smith did not interrupt him.

He put it back into the fire a fourth time to heat it for the piercing of the shaft hole. He waited until it glowed almost yellow before he removed it. Then, being careful to make the hole exactly in the center, he drove a small punch through the metal, then a larger one, and finally the shaft form. The shaft form was exactly the size of the wooded shaft which would make the handle of the adz and was tapered.

The metal was cooling, and Jacob knew he had to work fast before it welded itself to the form. With quick firm taps, he beat the edges into a uniform, round, smooth shape. When he was satisfied he gave the form a sharp rap and popped it free.

There sat the red hot adz. He was proud of it. *It is well formed, if I have to say so myself.*

But the trickiest part of the job remained. An adz had to be carefully tempered. The edge must be tempered very hard so it would take and retain an edge while the shaft end must be tempered as soft as possible so it would absorb the blows without cracking. And the temper of the remaining metal betwixt the two ends must transition smoothly and uniformly from one temper to the other.

A hard temper required a quick cool while a soft temper required a slow cool. He told Hannah to stop pumping the bellows and carefully positioned the adz so the edge would cool while the heel would remain hot. He watched the color of the iron carefully. The smith had drilled him repeatedly to be aware of and understand the colors of iron and various types of steel; each hue represented a given temperature. The correct tempers could only be achieved by maintaining the correct temperatures the correct lengths of time. He very carefully eased the tool from the fire as it went through its stages. Finally, when only the heel was still glowing a dull blue, he pulled it from the fire. It was time to stamp the smith's mark into the yet pliable iron.

"A good tradesman always marks his creations," the smith had taught him, "for a good tradesman always guarantees his work. Only by marking it may he be sure a damaged tool is his own. Besides, marking one's work motivates a man to always do his best work." Thus everything made by the smith bore his stamp; a 'W' surrounded by sparks.

But the stamp was not at the base of the anvil where it belonged. Jacob searched for it frantically. The iron would not remain pliable for long. He knew the stamp had been there; he had put it there himself earlier. He spotted Mr. Wallace watching him.

"I canna find the stamp," he cried.

"It is here in my hand," said the smith calmly.

"Give it to me."

"Nae. Ah did nae make that adz; I'll nae have my mark upon it." He held out his left hand. "Make yer own mark." In his hand was a bright new stamp.

Jacob took it from him in wonder, and gazed at the design on the end. It was a tiny backward 'JS' within a Star of David; JS for Jacob Schram, and the Star of David which identified him as a Jew. Mr. Wallace knew Jacob was proud of being a Jew.

He looked at the smith in astonished gratitude. "Yeh made me my own stamp?"

"Aye," Mr. Wallace growled. "Yeh'd best use it before yer adz cools."

Jacob quickly clamped the tool, positioned his new stamp against the still hot heel, and gave it a hard rap with a hammer. When he took it away there was his mark in all its glory. He knew now what the smith had meant about a mark motivating a man to always do his best. This mark would forever identify this tool as his work; he would not want it to prove flawed.

With a welling heart he turned to thank Mr. Wallace but found him halfway to the door. "Best fit her shaft whilst it is warm," his master said.

Jacob selected a strong length of ash, shaped it quickly with a drawing knife, and smoothed it with a bit of glass. He slid it through the hole in the adz, and smacked it hard against the anvil several times to drive them together. He tested its balance and turned it from side to side to judge its dimensions. He was pleased.

"It is very nice," he heard the girl say. He had forgotten she was there. He glanced at her to find her smiling at him. He was arrested by her grey eyes. He was not sure what it was about them, a keen intelligence, a forceful will, what, but he found them both intriguing and intimidating. He dropped his gaze.

"If yeh pump the stone," he said to cover his embarrassment, "I'll sharpen it for yeh." He immediately regretted his suggestion; the stone was heavy and hard to pump, but the girl went willingly to it, got it spinning and began to pump.

Jacob sharpened the adz as quickly as he could while still doing a good job. He felt ashamed to work the girl so, but her pace never slackened until he was finished. Then she gave him another smile, thanked him, and left.

Jacob watched her walk through the leaves on the path. He was impressed. She had displayed strength and endurance he had not expected. He turned back into the smithy.

Mr. Wallace was heating a bar in the forge, and Jacob realized he had neglected to obtain a payment for the adz; he admitted as much to the smith.

His master waved it aside. "Her father'll pay me come Sunday," he said. He winked, and added, "Course Ah 'spec Ah'll eat more'n the value o' the adz at their table."

"Yeh'll eat at their table?"

"Every Sunday," he grunted, "ever since my missus died." He grinned at Jacob. "Hannah's mother fretted about me spendin' my Sundays alone."

So Hannah and her family were friends of his master. Jacob was not sure if it was a mark of trust or prudence that his master had chosen to make the first job he had delegated to him a task for a friend

"I dinna think a gal could work so hard."

"Gal?" the smith snorted, "Hannah is nae a gal!"

"What?"

Mr. Wallace shrugged. "Wheel," he admitted, "Ah reckon she be a lass. But she be unlike any lass yeh've 'ave met." He poked the embers and threw in a shovelful of coal. "Pump 'er a spell, will yeh?"

Jacob began to pump the bellows, and the smith ruminated, "Hannah be . . . wheel . . . Hannah be Hannah." He winked wickedly at Jacob. "Yeh'll understand when yeh commence to know 'er."

"Commence to know her? How shall I commence to know her? I am with the Gerbers whenever I am not working."

"Aye, wheel," laughed the smith. "I've a notion she'll find cause to visit us from time to time." He smirked out the side of his eye at Jacob. "Less Ah miss my guess, yeh've caught 'er eye."

Jacob stopped pumping. "What?!"

"Aye," said Mr. Wallace soberly. "And t'would be only fair to warn yeh . . . when Hannah charts a course . . . she rarely veers from it." He pursed his lips. "Generally 'cause she gains her destination."

"But . . . but . . ." Jacob did not know what to say. He sometimes could not tell when his master was serious and when he was teasing. This was one of those times. "She is but a gal. How old be she, twelve, thirteen?"

"Wheel now let me think," said the smith. Serious or joking he was clearly enjoying himself. "Ah recollect she 'ad a birthday not so very long ago. 'Ow old did she say she was?"

Jacob must have made an impatient sound, for his master turned merry eyes upon him, and said, "It'll come to me." He turned the iron bar in the fire carefully. "Aye tha' be it." He nodded his head decisively. "She be a wee past eleven."

"Eleven," Jacob cried. "I'm fourteen."

Mr. Wallace nodded his head approvingly. "I was three years senior my missus." He winked at Jacob. "Three years is trivial twixt mates."

"Twixt . . ." Jacob was again speechless. After thinking a moment, he said, "It may be trivial twixt mates but I wager yeh did not court yer missus when she was eleven."

"Nae, Ah did nae. Yeh'd win that wager." The smith took the bar out, and began to beat it into an arc. After several moments, he paused, and said, "But Ah was nae suggestin' yeh court Hannah." He resumed pounding.

Jacob waited until he finished, and thrust the iron back into the fire to reheat. "Glad I am to hear yeh say it."

"Nae," said his master placidly, "I spec Hannah'll do the courtin'."

"What?"

The smith considered him soberly. "Aye. Did nae Ah say she be unlike any lass yeh'd 'ave met?"

6   A Shooting Lesson

November, 1768

Jacob sat staring over the pond beside which he had agreed to meet Mr. Wallace. The pond was roughly halfway betwixt the smithy and the Gerbers. He was not sure which he was more excited about: the chance to fire a gun, or the opportunity to introduce his brother to his master. He was proud of Mateo, and anticipated having Mr. Wallace meet him.

It was a crisp autumn day, and Jacob allowed its peace and life to flow into him while Mateo went poking about the pond reeds. Jacob always felt more alive in the forests, and his Sundays with Mateo were nearly always spent roaming them.

There came a clap upon his back that nearly sent him sprawling, and a, "Ho there, Jacob." It was Mr. Wallace. "We be well met. Be that yer brother? What be his name again?"

"His name is Matt," Jacob said, trying to conceal his surprise. He was annoyed he had not noticed his master's approach.

Mateo came running, and cried, "Hey, Mr. Wallace," as if he'd known him for years.

Jacob envied the boy his easy way with strangers. Then he saw his master was not alone; Hannah was with him.

Why is she? He scowled. He had been looking forward to this time learning to shoot; why had he brought Hannah?

The memory of the teasing his master had given him after she had left rose up and made him feel awkward around her. *It had been teasing, had it not; surely she did not truly . . . But what if she did?*

A distressing thought came: what if his master was trying to involve him with her? Why else would he have brought her to their meeting?

Then he saw Mr. Wallace carried two weapons; one upon each shoulder while Hannah carried a third. *Ah, that must be it; he needed help carrying the guns.*

"I thank yeh for inviting me, Mr. Wallace," he heard his brother say. *Those are nearly all the English words he knows,* Jacob thought, laughing to himself. *And he only knows them because I taught him them on the way.* He wondered how Mr. Wallace would like trying to teach a boy who could not speak English to shoot. He would soon find out.

He realized he had not yet greeted Hannah, and that he was being rude. He glanced at her, and found her regarding him calmly with her un-nerving grey eyes. He forced himself to smile and say, "Hey, Hannah. Glad I am to see yeh." She did not answer, only smiled, and nodded.

The smith led them to a fallen branch, and carefully leaned his weapons against it. Jacob saw two were muskets and the third was a rifle. The man clapped Mateo on the back as if they were old friends.

"Matt, me laddie," he cried, "T'is glad Ah be to meet thee"

"He . . . he does not speak English," Jacob reminded him.

"Aye, aye," his master said, waving it aside. "Twill be no matter." He put his arm around Hannah, and pulled her forward. "Ah brought Hannah along to teach yeh how to handle a gun whilst I teach yer brother."

"H..Hannah?"

"Aye! Did nae Ah tell thee, Hannah be an old hand with guns; she and Ah've been shootin' together for years." He grinned down upon her. "She shot her first deer this past summer."

Jacob looked at her with new respect. Then he remembered the smith had said they had been shooting for years and was suddenly jealous.

This is ridiculous; I have only just met Mr. Wallace, why should I be jealous of what he and Hannah did before we met?

Nonetheless, he was. He was even more jealous when Mr. Wallace led Mateo away to one side of the pond while he had to follow Hannah to the other. Why couldn't Hannah teach Mateo?

Still, it is not Hannah's fault. "I'm glad yeh came to teach me to shoot," he lied.

She shot him a pert look, and smiled. "Yer welcome." She stopped in a small glade. "This shall suit. Now watch." She set the musket upon its stock, and uncorked the powder horn. Jacob watched her fill the cap with powder. "The cap is yer measure," she said, "put in neither more nor less." She carefully poured it down the muzzle. Then she withdrew the ramrod from its rings beneath the barrel, slid it down the muzzle, and then lifted and dropped it several times. "Yeh must tamp the powder firm."

She stuck the ramrod under her arm, opened the shot bag, and withdrew a ball and a small linen patch. Placing the ball in the exact center of the patch, she pushed them both into the muzzle and then, taking the ramrod, pushed them home. She again lifted the rod up and thrust it down until it bounced back a few times. She then replaced the ramrod in its rings under the muzzle and raised the musket level.

"Now we must prime her." She pulled the flintlock up and back until it clicked, then took a second horn, uncorked it, and measured a small bit of powder which she poured into the flash pan. Jacob saw the second powder was much finer than had been the first.

Then, making very sure Jacob was watching, she pulled back the flintlock, pulled the trigger, and eased the flintlock down until it rested upon the flash pan.

"The gun is now loaded," she said. She tilted the musket. "Yeh can see that the flintlock as it is contains the primer; yeh need not fear spilling it." She looked him in the eye. "Did yeh understand everything I did?" When he nodded, she asked, "Could yeh do it?" When he again nodded, she smiled.

She really is rather pretty when she smiles. Her eyes no longer bothered him.

"Good," she said, "then watch carefully." She pulled the flintlock back until it again locked, raised the musket to her shoulder, and lifted it level. Her cheek caressed it and, **Ker-blam**, it fired, and a dark hole appeared on a tree some ten yards distant.

She handed the weapon to Jacob, and slid the two horns and the shot bag from her shoulders. "Yer turn."

Jacob was again intensely aware of her grey eyes watching him as he went through the steps just as she had shown him. He was rewarded by a wide grin when he held the loaded weapon to her.

"Very good. Now, pick a tree, and shoot it."

From across the pond they heard a shot. That little rascal, Mateo, had beaten him to it.

He cocked the weapon, put it to his shoulder, and tried to aim it.

"No, no," she laughed. "Yer holding it all wrong. Here." She reached up, and tried to adjust it. "Yeh're too tall. Kneel down so I can see."

He knelt, and she came beside him and pushed the gun into the hollow of his shoulder, moved his left hand to where she wanted it, and pulled his head down and over to cradle the musket. Her touch was patient, gentle, but insistent.

"There. Now, sight along the barrel at a tree." She squatted behind him so she could also sight along it. "Now," she said very quietly, her mouth so close he could feel her breath on the back of his neck. "Do not jerk the trigger; squeeze it gently. It should be a surprise to yeh when it fires."

He gently squeezed. **Ker-blam!** It was a surprise, he had to resist the impulse to jump, and a gash appeared on the side of the tree. He felt her body suddenly upon his back, her arms flung about his shoulders, and her cheek against his own. "Oh very well done." Then she thrust herself away.

He turned, and grinned at her. Her intimacy had astonished him, but he couldn't say it had been unpleasant. She refused to meet his gaze; was that a blush he saw?

"It was very good for a first time," she muttered. "I've never seen anyone do so well before."

"How many others have yeh taught to shoot?" he demanded.

She looked up, and her eyes flashed, but then she grinned. "Yeh be my first."

For some reason the exchange broke the reserve which had been betwixt them, and they both laughed.

"I am surprised yer parents allowed yeh to come alone with Mr. Wallace," Jacob said. This had been bothering him since their arrival. What kind of parents would allow a young girl to go unescorted into the forest with a man?

She shrugged. "Why should they not? He is my uncle."

"Yer uncle? But . . . But I thought . . ." Jacob stepped back a step, and regarded her. "Mr. Wallace told me he has neither sisters nor brothers."

"No more has he."

"Then how. . ."

"Ah!" She scowled at him. "The same way Matt is yer brother."

He was shocked and dismayed. "Yeh know Matt is not my real brother?"

"He is yer real brother," she scoffed. "Yeh merely had different parents."

While Jacob digested that comment she patiently continued. "Blood cannot make a real brother; neither can the lack thereof prevent one. If two people choose to be related, then they be."

Jacob stared at her. *She is right, but most people would never perceive it thus. But I don't believe she cares if anyone else perceives it or agrees with her; she knows she is right, and that is sufficient.*

With a sudden insight he understood why her calm gaze had been disconcerting; she had not cared what he thought of her. Her only concern had been her opinion of him.

Mr. Wallace was right, she is unlike any lass I have ever met.

"Yeh want to shoot again?" she asked.

"May I?"

She nodded. "As often as yeh please."

As if to confirm her statement, there came the report of a second shot from across the pond. Mateo was again ahead of him.

While he reloaded the musket she asked, "What do yeh and Matt usually do of a Sunday?"

"Nothin'," he muttered. He wished she would not ask him questions; he didn't want to make a mistake. But when he glanced at her, he saw she was dismayed, and paused. He caught her eye, and grinned. "Nothing important that is; mostly just roam the forest."

To his relief, she smiled back, and asked, "Yeh like the forest?" When he nodded, she said, "So do I."

She said no more, and he returned to his reloading, but no sooner had he done so than he heard her say, "There is an Injin who lives to the north. My cousins used to go and see him of a weekend."

Jacob felt a stab of annoyance, but then laughed. *Perhaps she is talking deliberately, to see if I can reload the musket with a distraction.* He determined he would prove he could.

"This Injin taught my cousins all sorts o' things about the forest.

"Uh-mum." Jacob drove the ball home, and bounced the rod before replacing it in its rings.

"I'm sure he lives there still," she continued. "I'll bet he'd teach yeh and yer brother, were yeh to ask him."

That caught Jacob's attention. He had yet to meet a real Indian; to be taught by one would be wonderful. He set the musket down carefully, and regarded her. "Do yeh really think he would?"

She was watching him calculatingly. "Aye," she said slowly. "Course yeh'd have to take me with yeh."

"Why?"

"To . . . to . . . introduce yeh." Her eyes blazed. "Think yeh he'd teach yeh without an introduction?"

Jacob had to resist scoffing at her. *That's not the real reason.* "Does he know yeh?"

Her eyes dropped. "Nae." But then she looked up with open pleading in her eyes. "Please take me with yeh. I've wanted to go and see him for ever so long; but my parents will not allow me to go so far alone."

"How far is he?"

"Ten miles, more or less."

Ten miles isn't so far. Still, he could understand her parents forbidding her from going alone. He wasn't sure he would allow Mateo to go so far into the forest alone. He raised the musket to his shoulder, took a careful aim, and fired. He was distressed to find the hole in the tree was a good seven inches from where he had aimed.

He began again to reload and said, "Yer parents would not allow yeh to accompany me; they do not know me."

She waited until he was nearly finished before saying, "They could learn to know yeh."

He glanced up at her, and shook his head. He was not going to meet her parents. He carefully primed the musket.

"Mr. Wallace could vouch for yeh. They'd trust his judgment."

He did not reply, only hefted the weapon to his shoulder and again carefully took aim. **Ker-blam.** Again the shot was off; this time high.

"Tarnation, I am a lousy shot!" At least he had beaten his brother this time; he had fired his third shot before him.

"Yeh are not," she said stoutly. "Did not yeh hit the tree all three times?"

"Aye," he admitted with a smile, "only because she is a large tree. But look how far apart they be."

"That is about as good as yeh can expect from a musket, Jacob, my lad," said the smith. Jacob spun around to find his master and brother standing and watching him. Again he had snuck up behind him without his notice.

"How do yeh do that?" he gasped.

"Do what?"

"Sneak up behind me like that."

Mr. Wallace roared with laughter. "Ach! Tis sorry I be," he finally managed to say. "I did nae mean to sneak up upon yeh. Tis only it be my habit to walk with stealth in the forest." He winked at Jacob, took the musket from his hands, and replaced it with the rifle. "Tis one o' th' things ol' Woosamequin'll teach yeh I spec."

"Woosamequin?"

"The ol' Injin Hannah told yeh about."

"So yeh agree Woosamequin would agree to teach 'em," Hannah said excitedly.

"Aye." Mr. Wallace laughed. "I expect he'd jump at the chance to take 'em under his wing. Likely he's tired o' sittin' about his daughter's house."

"And I'd be allowed to go with them, wouldn't I?" she demanded. "Yeh'd vouch for 'em wouldn't yeh?"

"One thing at a time, lassie. Let's give Jacob a go at shootin' the rifle."

To Jacob's surprise, she fell silent. He looked over the rifle, and then glanced at the smith. "Do I load it the same way as the musket?"

"Precisely the same," he answered. "O' course yeh use the rifle's powder horns and balls."

Jacob nodded, and carefully loaded the rifle. He was very aware of the trio's eyes upon him, but was rewarded by a grin from his master when he held the loaded weapon to him.

"Yeh did it exactly right."

The smith patted Hannah upon the shoulder, and said to her, "Well done."

He turned back to Jacob. "Go ahead and sight her. Yeh'll find it easier since the barrel is nae round."

Jacob lifted the rifle to his cheek, and saw how the barrel did indeed make it much easier to aim. The barrel was hexagonal, and he could sight straight down one of the edges. He picked one of his musket holes, did his best to line it up, and squeezed the trigger. **Ker-blam**. His shoulders drooped.

"I'm nae better with the rifle than I was with the musket."

"Nonsense, my lad," said the smith. He was looking at him with respect. "Yeh're a natural. That was very well shot."

"But," protested Jacob, "the shot is three inches to the left and two below where I aimed."

"Aye," replied the smith. He took the rifle, and quickly reloaded it. "Yeh'll remember I told yeh every rifle has its own personality. This one shoots to the left and low just as yeh said. But, unlike a musket, which never shoots twice the same way, a rifle shall shoot exactly the same every time." He handed the loaded weapon back to Jacob. "Try 'er again. Aim her exactly as yeh did before."

Jacob obeyed and, to his joy, found his new ball hit within an inch of his former one. Hannah clasped her hands, and fairly danced, and Mateo whooped. Mr. Wallace took the rifle from Jacob, and put one hand upon his shoulder. Jacob saw he was staring at him with awe.

"Yeh were born to shoot, Jacob. Yeh'll make a name for yerself someday."

Jacob stared at his feet. "T'was nothing."

"D'nae kid yerself. Taint a man in a thousand could do as well, particularly upon their first day." He glanced at the sun. "I wish we had time for Matt and Hannah to shoot the rifle a spell, but we'll soon lose our light. There'll be other days." He led them back to the road.

There they said their goodbyes but, before they parted, Hannah again asked Mr. Wallace, "Do yeh nae think my parents shall allow me to accompany Jacob and Matt to see Woosamequin."

The smith scratched his cheek, and finally grinned. "Were yeh any other gal, I'd say nae. But I've learned nae to underestimate yer powers o' persuasion."

"And yeh'll vouch for Jacob and Matt?"

"Aye. Iffin yeh be in their company, yeh'd have naught to fear."

Jacob saw a brief scowl cross her face. She did not like the implication that she needed his protection.

Not that I blame her. I would not like it were I her. But she is a girl.

For the first time he wondered if that mattered as much as he had always thought. Could it be a girl could value her independence as much as he did?

Clearly Hannah did, and he found himself respecting her for it.

7   For Pity's Sake

November, 1768

"Jacob," his master asked the following Wednesday, "would yeh like to learn to shoot the rifle; competitively that is?" They had just unloaded a large shipment of iron and were taking one of his master's frequent beer breaks.

"Shoot competitively?"

"Aye." His master tore a hunk of bread from the loaf. "There is a multitude o' competitions about; especially this time o' year when there is little else a man can do." He grinned. "Ah've tried my hand in my time, but," he shrugged, "me hand was ne'er steady enough."

He shook the bread at Jacob. "Yer hand be steady as a rock and yeh've a keen eye. Ah seen yeh shoot, an Ah know talent when Ah see it."

He considered Jacob. "Ah know everything there be concernin' shootin'; be yeh willin' to learn, twixt my experience an' yer talent, yeh'd be a force to contend with. What d'yeh say?"

Jacob hardly knew what to say. But he knew he enjoyed shooting, and would welcome an excuse to do more of it. And the thought of competing against other men and boys and perhaps excelling was appealing. He grinned, and answered, "I'd like that."

"Very good," his master cried. "We'll make time to get in a bit o' trainin' every day then. There be a turkey shoot west o' here in a month's time. I expect yeh'll be ready fer it." His eyes gleamed. "There be a few men I relish seein' yeh beat."

Jacob looked forward to the training, but it reminded him of the other training he anticipated; the training the old Indian could give. He had expected every day for the smith to inform him that he had spoken with Hannah's parents, and a trip to see the old Indian was planned, but the days had slipped by without such an announcement. He asked the smith about it.

His master seemed strangely reluctant to speak of it, but, after several proddings said, "There is nae reason yeh and yer brother can nae go by yerselves. Ah could direct yeh; yeh'd easily find 'im."

Jacob's heart surged. So he could go and see the Indian whether Hannah could go or not? He had wanted to meet a real Indian for years. And, he admitted, he would enjoy it much better without Hannah. Not that he disliked her, it was just . . . her presence would hinder the free and easy comradre he and Mateo enjoyed when they were alone together.

He and the smith returned to the workshop. "Will yeh tell me this Friday so we can go this Sunday?"

"Friday," grunted his master, "Ah'll tell thee now. Twill nae be difficult to remember. Yeh simply travel due north till yeh reach th' river. Yeh'll find the Injin's camp somewhere upon its banks; I disremember whether east or west, but yeh'll easily discover it by a bit o' searchin'."

Jacob nodded soberly, but he felt as excited as a child. In only a few days, he and Mateo were going to visit a real Indian! Hopefully he would agree to teach them the ways of the forest.

But then he remembered the pleading he had seen in Hannah's eyes, and his excitement waned. She desired to visit the old Indian at least as much as he did; how could he enjoy himself knowing he had left her behind?

He waited until his master had selected the iron he desired and plunged it into the fire before asking, "So . . . Hannah cannot go."

The smith frowned, and did not reply for several moments. Finally he growled, "It nae be fittin' fer her to be runnin' th' woods. S'different fer yeh and yer brother."

Jacob was surprised. It was true he would have considered it inappropriate for most girls but, as his master had said himself, Hannah was not like most girls. For one thing, most girls would not desire to run the woods. Besides had he not also said Hannah had been hunting with him for years? Was that not running the woods?

"I do not believe yeh mean that."

His master glared at him, but did not deny it.

"What is the true reason she cannot go? Did her parents not accept yer voucher o' me?"

The smith did not reply, only yanked his metal from the fire, and began to beat it. Finally he stopped, and turned his back upon his work to stare Jacob in the eye. "Ah did nae vouch fer yeh."

"Yeh didn't?"

"Nae."

Jacob's heart sank, and he stared at the floor. His master did not trust him?

"T'was nae yeh," the smith said. Jacob looked back at him. "T'was me. Or rather t'was the lad Ah was at fourteen." He grinned apologetically. "Ah would nae trust the lad Ah was with a gal in the forest fer a day." He glanced away, and ran his fingers through his hair before turning back to Jacob. "Yeh are nae the lad Ah was; were Hannah my daughter, Ah'd trust yeh with her, but . . . she is nae my daughter, and to go to another man and give him guarantee his lass'd be safe . . ." He again ran his fingers through his hair. "That Ah can nae do." He stared Jacob in the eye. "Ah can nae be that sure."

Jacob nodded. He could understand that.

So there it was; Hannah could not go. It was not his fault. He felt happy again.

But only for a moment. Was it really true it was not his fault she could not go? Was there nothing he could do to make it possible?

He remembered Hannah's suggestion he could mayhap meet her parents, and he groaned. That he definitely did not want to do. But he found himself asking his master if he could arrange it.

* * * *

Jacob sat in the parlor of Hannah's house, and gazed around himself in awe. She lived in a real house, not a log cabin; it had two stories and a parlor. It was true it was simply furnished but it was a house and indicated a wealth he had not suspected of her.

Her father entered the room, and sat in a chair across from him.

"Why, I would ask, do yeh desire to take Hannah along with yeh to visit Woosamequin? Yeh do not need her aid."

Jacob tried to think of a good reason why he needed her to go, but Hannah's father had the same steel grey eyes she possessed and they seemed able to read his every thought. He decided he could only tell the truth.

"Begging yer pardon sir, but I do not. I do not need her aid, and I do not desire her company.

"No offense intended, sir," he hastened to add. "Yer daughter is a fine gal." He stared at his feet. "But my brother and I, we value our solitude."

He looked back at Hannah's father who arched an eyebrow. "Then why have yeh come asking me to allow her to accompany yeh?"

"Because," Jacob said dejectedly, "I know how very much she desires to accompany us, t'was she who told me of Woosamequin, t'would be unfair to go without 'er."

Hannah's father regarded him for several moments. "So yeh're troubling yerself to obtain her company though yeh do not desire it?"

Jacob shrugged miserably. He had known this meeting would be embarrassing and difficult.

Her father laughed, and leaned forward. "I'll thank yeh to nae allow Hannah to know that." He leaned back, and smiled. "Hannah has church on Sunday which she shall nae miss, but, if yeh and yer brother are here at ten, she'll skip her dinner and go with yeh." He winked. "I'll ensure her mother has packed enough in a basket to feed the three o' yeh."

Jacob looked up surprised. So she could go. He liked Hannah's father. And having a basket of food provided them would compensate for having her accompany them. He thought about saying so, but could not think of a way to say it without sounding rude. Besides, he believed Hannah's father already knew.

He rose, thanked the man, and made his escape. He ran home to the Gerber's to tell his brother the news. He could hardly wait for Sunday to come.

8 Woosamequin

November, 1768

Jacob, Mateo, and Hannah worked their way toward yet another bend in the river. The river had been easy enough to find, and their walk to it had been swift, for they had merely had to follow the trail which led north until it had crossed it. But the trio had had to choose to go either down the river or up; there had been no way of knowing which was correct.

They had chosen down the river.

After a spell they had concluded they had chosen incorrectly.

An hour and a half later they had returned to the ford and begun the trek upstream. The problem with following a river along its bank was that brush often grew nearly into the water. Jacob was growing very weary of forcing his way through it. He was sure the others were also.

But of course Mateo, despite being so young, was as tough as a mule. Jacob was not surprised to find him still smiling; sometimes he believed the little imp enjoyed adversity.

It was Hannah he had begun to worry about. Would her endurance hold? They still had to make the trek home again. What would her father say if he returned her exhausted? Yet, though she showed evidence she would be as thankful as he to escape the brush, she had yet to show signs of flagging and her spirits appeared high.

The excitement she had displayed when they had left her house had been amusing. But, unlike most girls of Jacob's acquaintance, her excitement had not caused her to chatter. In fact, he found her as quiet as a boy.

Her presence did dampen the free comradre he and Mateo always enjoyed, but not nearly as much as Jacob had expected. In fact, in some ways, as the three grew more comfortable with one another, she added a dimension. He was now glad she was with them.

They rounded the bend. and there, finally, was the Indian village. It did not look like much, five cabins tucked in trees with open land between them where gardens had been in the summer. He noticed a nice wide trail leading south from the village, and determined they would follow it when they left; it was bound to be a quicker and more direct route.

The cabins themselves looked very like white men's cabins, but the children running about were clearly Indian, and the trio was quickly spied and surrounded.

Jacob had seen Indians from a distance before, but never close. Now he found himself marveling at the beauty of their skin. They were called 'red men' but they were not red; they were a rich golden bronze, and their eyes and hair were both raven black.

For a moment he felt intimidated by the dozen brown faces staring up at him, but asked, "Does Woosamequin live here?" *Do these children even speak English?*

Clearly they at least recognized the name for, though none of them replied, they all ran toward a cabin beckoning the trio to follow.

At the door Jacob hesitated. Should he knock? Did Indians knock?

The children negated the question by yelling, "Woosamequin," followed by a stream of words. *So that is the Indian tongue,* Jacob thought. He liked the sound of it; wild and melodious. He wanted to learn it. He had always enjoyed learning new words.

The door opened, and there before them stood Woosamequin. It had to be him; his hair had many silver strands mingled with the black and was very long; it hung about his shoulders and half way down his back. But his face, except around his eyes, was unlined and his eyes were clear and commanding. He did not stand like an old man either; he stood straight, strong, and proud. He was rather intimidating until he smiled.

"Visitors. And young ones at that." He stepped back, and held the door open. "Come in."

Jacob entered, followed by his brother, Hannah, and every child outside the door. Evidently the children considered themselves welcome. The cabin had no chairs or benches, but there were mats upon the floor, and the children crowded upon them until Woosamequin scolded them, and one was relinquished for the visitors.

Jacob sat cross legged upon it as he saw the children do, and Mateo crowded against one side while Hannah sat on the other. It was rather snug, but . . . also rather pleasant.

Woosamequin settled himself upon his own mat, and asked, "What has brought yeh to my door?"

Jacob was unsure what to say. *How do you ask a stranger if he shall train you in the ways of the forest? Why should he, we have nothing to offer him.* Suddenly the idea seemed very presumptuous.

But Hannah was not so reserved. "We have come to ask yeh to train us in the Indian ways; in the ways of the forest."

To Jacob's relief, the old man seemed more amused than offended.

"Why did yeh come to me?"

"Yeh trained my cousins," Hannah said. "Ten years or so ago."

Woosamequin leaned back against the wall, and considered her. "Yer cousins?"

"Aye. Squire and Daniel. Do yeh remember them?"

"Squire and Daniel." The old man's eyes lit up. "Ah yes, the Boone boys. What a pair they were." He grinned at Hannah. "So yeh're a Boone gal?"

"Nae. Their mother and my mother were sisters. I'm an O'Malley."

The old Indian nodded. "And these are yer brothers?"

Hannah giggled.

Jacob glanced at her in surprise. She was acting so . . . well, like a girl.

But then, she is a girl.

"No," Hannah said, "They are my friends, Jacob and Matt Schram. My name is Hannah." She smiled prettily. "So will yeh train us?"

Woosamequin did not reply, only scratched his chin.

"Please do. We'd be ever so grateful, and we'd work very hard." She stopped, and her shoulders sagged. "Yeh trained them."

A slow sad smile spread over the old man's face. "That was nearer twenty years ago than ten. And my legs are not what they used to be."

Jacob felt Hannah wilt beside him. Without a thought, he put his arm around her, and held her.

Woosamequin stared at them, and then sighed and asked, "Can yeh follow directions and obey 'em"

Hannah perked up. "Aye."

"Can yeh each find yer way through the woods without gettin' yerself lost?"

"Aye."

He sat for a few long moments. Even the Indian children seemed to be holding their breaths. "I'll teach yeh on two conditions. First, yeh'll have my grandson, Philip, join yeh. He needs to be taught, but the things he needs to learn can only be learned in a group. Yeh'll be his group."

Philip? Jacob thought. That did not seem like an Indian name. He was a little disappointed.

"Agreed," Hannah said triumphantly.

"Mayhap yeh should meet him before yeh agree." The old man grinned. "For that matter, we should allow him to meet yeh; he may not wish to join yeh." He hove himself to his feet, and led them to the door. Outside he said a few words, and the children reluctantly abandoned them. He led the trio toward the stream.

"Do yeh always allow the gal to speak for yeh?" he asked Jacob.

Jacob blushed, but answered, "Gals are better at convincing than boys."

The old man laughed. "That they be."

At the river they found Philip weaving a basket. Jacob guessed him to be ten years old.

Hannah surprised Philip by dropping beside him and demanding he show her how he was making the basket, but Jacob could tell it pleased him to comply. Did Hannah have no self consciousness? Did she just assume everyone she met would like her? It seemed she did.

It also seemed she was right.

Woosamequin explained his intention to train Philip with the three, and the boy agreed.

"Were yeh intending to come on Sundays?" Woosamequin asked Jacob.

"Aye. If that be suitable."

"Every Sunday?"

"If we may."

The man nodded. "My second condition be that yeh shall each bring a fresh rabbit when yeh come each week."

"A rabbit? But . . . but how are we to obtain . . . I'm not sure we can do that."

Woosamequin waved his protestations aside. "I shall teach yeh how to snare them. Be we agreed?"

Jacob grinned. "Agreed."

The Indian nodded. "But first, we'll play the game we'll play 'most every week. It'll teach yeh more than anything else I could do, and also show me what yeh need the most work on. Come." All four followed him back to his cabin.

When they were seated in an arc facing him, Woosamequin said, "I'll have one among yeh volunteer to go into the forest alone. He shall have a five minute head start. Then the other three shall track and attempt to capture him. His task shall be to elude them. In any case yeh shall all return here in one hour." The creases around his eyes crinkled. "Who shall be my volunteer? Yeh'll all get a chance from week to week."

Jacob whispered what he had said to Mateo in German, and the boy raised his hand.

Woosamequin frowned, and said, "I asked for a volunteer, not a recruit. If I'm to teach yeh, yeh shall be equals."

Jacob explained, "I did not tell him to volunteer, I only translated what yeh had said. Matt does not understand English."

"He does not understand English?"

"No, but he is a very fast learner, and he is very perceptive." He began to worry Mateo would be rejected. "He can understand much more than yeh may think even if he does not understand yer words."

Woosamequin stared at the boy for a moment, and then ordered him to go.

Verifying Jacob's prediction, the boy ran and Woosamequin said, "Whilst yeh wait I'll teach yeh to walk."

Teach us to walk? Jacob laughed to himself. *What does he mean? I've known how to walk since I was a babe.*

But the man was serious. "Get up. Walk from the door to the far wall."

Jacob self consciously obeyed.

"Tsk, listen to how loud yeh be." "Yeh," he commanded Hannah. "Walk"

Hannah walked. She was much quieter, but could still be easily heard.

"Now watch Philip."

Philip walked across the room, and Jacob was amazed to find he heard nothing. He stared at him in amazement. But when he caught the boy's eye, and grinned at him, Philip glanced away in confusion.

Jacob realized he was shy.

"Sit," the old Indian commanded, and the three sat. "When yeh walk, do not slap yer feet like a duck." He rose, and demonstrated; exaggerating the slap of his feet upon the floor.

"Yer maker gave yer feet muscles and bones; he intended yeh to use them. Look."

To Jacob's astonishment, he removed one moccasin, and deliberately put his foot into the ash of the cold hearth. He then made a footprint upon the clean floor. Jacob wondered what his daughter would say when she saw it.

"When yeh step, yer entire foot should not hit the ground at the same time. Yeh should place yer heel upon the ground; not thump it. Then yer foot should roll forward shifting yer weight to its outer edge and finally back to the bones behind yer three large toes." His toe traced the imprint of his foot as he spoke. "By that point there should be no weight upon yer heel or outside of yer foot; they should already be coming off the ground. Then yer weight should shift to the toes and they should thrust yeh forward.

"Now get up, and walk again."

Jacob and Hannah obeyed. Jacob tried hard to follow the old man's instructions. He found he could do it, but he had to concentrate; if he stopped concentrating, he automatically fell back to his old way of walking. But when he did it right, his steps were silent.

"Shouldn't yeh have taught us this while Matt was here?" he asked.

Woosamequin waved his concern away. "This is something yeh can easily teach him. I want yeh all to practice it on yer way home. Do it until it becomes natural."

"Shouldn't we be chasing Matt? He's been gone much more than five minutes."

The old man chuckled. "Come." He led them out of the cabin, and to the top of a small hill. There they could see some distance in all directions. "Where is Matt?"

Jacob looked carefully all around them. *If there were snow, this would be easy.* But there was no snow; only the dried leaves of the fall. He saw no clue to tell him where his brother was, nor which way he had gone. He glanced back at Woosamequin, and shrugged. So did Hannah and Philip.

"Do not look at the ground," their teacher ordered. "Look at the birds. They're yer informants." He pointed to the northwest.

Jacob looked. He saw crows cawing above a small ravine. They were moving slowly away from them. "He is in that ravine?"

"Aye," said the old man cheerfully. "And where is he headed?"

Jacob scanned the terrain. He saw the ravine curved slowly to the right and eventually emptied into another ravine which led directly back to the village. He did not see any other exit unless his brother scaled an edge. But he did not think he would do so for he would then be exposed to their sight. He looked at Woosamequin with delight.

"He is going to that ravine. He intends to return here by it." Hannah agreed, and Philip nodded. The old man smiled.

"Run, and intercept him."

This the three did. Jacob very much enjoyed the look of surprise and frustration on his brother's face when he walked right into their ambush.

But by then it was quite late, and they had to hurry back to the village. On the way, Jacob tried to engage Philip in conversation, but found it difficult. With Hannah, however, the boy seemed free and easy.

Jacob allowed Hannah and Philip to precede he and Matt, and Philip became even more animated. Watching them, Jacob was both mystified and a little jealous. What magic did Hannah possess that she could make friends so easily?

Back at the village, they bid the old man and Philip goodbye, and departed. Woosamequin assured them the trail south would indeed be much quicker and shorter, and so it proved. Jacob not only got Hannah home before sunset, he and Matt made it halfway to the Gerbers in the light.

But then he remembered Woosamequin had failed to teach them how to snare a rabbit. *Well it cannot be helped. We'll have to figure it out for ourselves. It cannot be that hard.* He felt sure they could.

9 Speakin' Injin

November, 1768

Jacob and Mateo sat outside Hannah's house the following Sunday waiting for her and her family to return from church. At their feet lay three fresh rabbits. It had taken them several days to fashion effective ways to snare them; since they had wanted to be sure to have three fresh ones, they had set a dozen snares the evening before, and had caught seven rabbits. Martha had been happy to dispose of the four extra; there would be rabbit stew awaiting their return that evening.

"It's too bad we must waste half the day waiting for Hannah," Mateo said.

"Yes, it is," Jacob agreed. He also chaffed at the waste. The hours with the Indian were so valuable, it was distressing to waste half of the day. He grinned down upon his brother. "But it cannot be helped, can it? Such are the circumstances we must abide."

"Why?" His brother had his familiar mischievous glint in his eye.

"Hannah must attend church, and her parents will not allow her to go unless we accompany her. You would not want to leave her behind, would you?"

"No." Mateo's glint grew stronger. "But why cannot we go without her, and yet accompany her?"

"What do you mean?" Jacob asked, although he was beginning to suspect his brother's plan.

"We could go to Woosamequin's from the Gerbers in the morning. It wouldn't be much further than coming here. We could have several hours with him, and then come here for Hannah."

"You'd be willing to do all that extra walking?"

"Wouldn't you?"

Jacob would. He saw Hannah's family round the bend. He grinned down upon his brother. "If one of us gets a chance, we'll ask Woosamequin to allow it." He glanced at Hannah. "But we'll not allow Hannah to know, all right?"

His brother nodded.

* * * *

Hannah laughed when they showed her their three rabbits, and led them to a shed where she had three of her own hanging. "What shall we do with these?"

Jacob shrugged. "Couldn't yer mother use them?"

"Nae," she said. "She's gotten her fill o' rabbits." She eyed him coyly. "I had to test my snares, didn't I?"

"Give 'em all to Woosamequin," said Mateo.

Three weekends with Hannah and already he is beginning to understand and speak English. Jacob was proud of him.

"He is right," he said. "They can be pay for his lessons last week."

Hannah agreed, and they were soon on their way eating the generous meal her mother had packed in her basket.

Wosamiquin's face lit up when he saw they had brought not three rabbits, but six. He seemed to be in a jovial mood, and Jacob took the chance to teasingly chide him for neglecting to teach them how to snare them as he had promised.

"What do yeh mean?" the old man demanded. "Did yeh not learn to snare them?"

"Aye, but we had to do so on our own."

The creases around the man's eyes crinkled. "If yeh'll remember, I said I'd teach yeh to snare rabbits; I did not say I'd teach yeh how to do so."

Jacob did not know what to answer to that, and was silent.

"I forced yeh to figure out how to snare rabbits upon yer own," said Woosamequin, "and that skill shall be more valuable than learning what yeh're shown. It is not difficult to capture a rabbit; they're not very bright." He grinned. "I'll show yeh some excellent ways by and by. Likely they'll be better than the ways yeh contrived."

He eyed them sternly. "But learning the skill to contrive ways to do what must be done is a skill far more valuable than learning a particular type o' snare."

Philip arrived, and Woosamequin asked who would volunteer to be the prey in their game. This time Hannah lifted her hand and was sent out.

Jacob was glad. That gave him and Mateo plenty of time to ask Woosamequin privately if they could come in the morning Sundays.

The old Indian appraised them. "And what would yeh wish to do when yeh came?"

Jacob had been thinking of that on their way to see him, and was ready with an answer; both he and Mateo enjoyed learning new languages, and he desired to learn to speak Indian. "Would yeh teach us to speak Indian in the mornings? We'll be happy to bring yeh more rabbits if yeh desire."

The old Indian chuckled. "An old man is not what yeh need to learn to speak Wampanoag," he said. "The best teachers o' a language are children. If yeh wish to learn, my daughters'd be happy to allow yeh to tend to their children for a few hours of a morning." He winked at his grandson. "Wouldn't they, Philip?"

To Jacob's surprise, Philip was standing, scowling at him and Mateo.

Woosamequin directed a stream of Indian words at him, and Philip answered with the same, but then scowled at Jacob, and said, "I'm sure they would." He glanced at his grandfather, and then back at Jacob. "I'll go and arrange for them to play with yeh at dawn next week."

Jacob thanked him weakly, and the boy left.

Woosamequin watched him go, and then, with a false joviality, said, "It shan't take the children long to teach yeh."

Jacob did not understand what had transpired nor why, but decided to pretend he had noticed nothing. "Wampanoag?" he asked, "Be that what yeh call the Indian tongue?"

"It is what we speak. In truth, there are but a few Indians who speak Wampanoag any more." His face was suddenly tired and old, but then it cleared, and he added, "But all Indian languages are very similar. If yeh learn to understand Wampanoag, yeh'll be able to make yerself understood by most any Indian."

"Any Indian?"

"Aye. Of course the closer the tribe lives, the more similar their language'll be."

His eyes flared. "Except for the Iroquois. But the Iroquois are not Indian." His face grew hard. "They are snake men." He shook his head. "They speak an entirely different language, but yeh need never learn their language for the Iroquois are to be avoided at all cost."

"Where do the Iroquois live?"

"In the far northwest, thank the maker. But they have been known to make raids as far south and east as Berks county." The old man shuddered. "Some say they are not even human, but fiends in human form."

"Surely that is not true."

"Perhaps not." The old man shook his head. "But yeh've never seen the result of an Iroquois raid. Pray God yeh never do. Yeh are fortunate the English have gained and maintained an alliance with 'em. The Frenchies it are who have suffered their wrath."

He grinned at Jacob. "That was the only reason yeh won the war against the Frenchies and gained their territory."

Philip returned, and Woosamequin waved his hand at the door. "Enough talking. Hannah'll be back before yeh begin. Yeh'd best be on her trail."

10 The Shoot

February, 1769

Jacob watched the other shooters as he anxiously awaited his turn. His master had been drilling him nearly every day for the past month and a half, but he wished he had brought him to view a few matches before entering him in one. Still, the smith had assured him there was nothing to it; he'd quickly learn. Fortunately he was in the last tier of shooters.

There were thirty men and boys entered in the shoot, they shot five at a time. Jacob watched as each man took his place along a fence, were handed a six inch square of wood which they marked as they chose; most with an X, and signed or made their mark upon it. These squares were then given to boys who ran them down and placed them upon another fence thirty feet away.

Once the boys were clear, the signal was given to load the weapons. Each shooter loaded, and fired at will. When all had done so, the boys again ran to the targets and took them to a group of judges who carefully measured the accuracy of the shots, and recorded them.

The smith had told Jacob only the top one third of the shooters would be allowed to shoot again in the second round. Of those ten, only five would advance to the third round, only two to the fourth, and of course the winner of the fourth would win the turkey.

"Yeh'll be that winner," he had assured him.

It was Jacob's turn to shoot but, as he stepped to the fence, his master came to speak into his ear. "Jacob, my lad, there be only five who've shot closer than three inches from their mark. Thus, Ah'll have yeh place yer shot nae closer than that"

"Why?"

"Three inches'll get yeh into the next round." His master's eyes glinted. "Do nae shoot better than yeh have to." He slapped Jacob upon the back. "Step up to the line."

Jacob did so and took his square of wood. But, as he carefully marked it with a large X, he watched his master. He handed the square to the boy who ran it to the other fence.

Jacob's master was surrounded by friends who were asking him about the new boy he had brought; was he any good?

"Aye," the smith said with a grin. "He is fair ta midlin'. I spec he'll hold 'is own."

"Yeh believe he'll make it into the next round?"

"Aye. There be a good chance he shall."

"Yeh wouldn't be willin' to venture a wager upon it would yeh?"

Jacob watched with amusement as his master seemed to consider the proposition for a moment before replying he might be persuaded to do so. So that was why he had told Jacob to shoot only well enough to qualify for the next round; he intended to raise the odds against him for the next round of bets.

When the order came to load and shoot, he took his time loading, not only because the smith had taught him that careful loading was the most important part of accurate shooting, but because he wanted to allow his competition to fire first.

Only nine of the former twenty five have shot closer than five inches. If none of the four now beat them, I need only get within that limit.

One by one they shot, and still Jacob dawdled. It would not be bad to allow his master's friends to believe he was an inept loader. He carefully evaluated the others' shots. Two were well beyond five inches; one had been a clean miss, but one he judged to be at four and three quarters. He resolved to aim for three and a half inches. He was confident he would not be off by more than an inch; he would yet have a quarter inch to spare.

He lifted the rifle to his cheek, held his breath for a moment as his master had taught him, and fired. He was pleased with his shot; if it was not at four inches, he'd eat straw for his supper.

When the squares had been measured, his shot was announced to be three and seven eights. *I'll still not eat straw*, Jacob grinned to himself; *their measure could be off that much*.

His master met him as he came from the fence. His hands were filled with coins. "Very well done, my boy," he whispered with a wink, "very well done indeed." He pressed a handful of coins into Jacob's hand before returning to his pals. Jacob heard his friends ask if he thought his boy could survive the next round.

The smith grinned at Jacob, and said he would.

"Be yeh willing ta wager upon him?"

Jacob watched in astonishment as his master thumped his remaining coins upon a plank, and announced he'd meet any and all takers. There were many who took him up upon it.

Jacob was assigned to the second set of five shooters. He watched as the first five shot; four of them made exceptionally fine shots. Even the fifth had made a good shot. Everyone knew it would take a very fine shot from one of the second five to unseat him. Jacob listened as his master's friends jeered him, saying they bet he regretted placing so much money upon his lad.

The smith calmly reached into his pocket, pulled out a pound note, and laid it upon the plank. "I'll bet he'll nae only be in the next round," he announced, "he'll make it into the fourth." He looked around challengingly. "Be there any who'll bet he'll nae?" There was a rush of takers, and the pound soon had ten or twenty across from it.

Jacob was a little nervous to have so much money riding upon him, but took his best shot; an inch and a quarter; easily good enough to pass to the next round.

Now he faced five shooters; all grown men. His master had won his second bet, but the big one, where he was risking a pound, remained. Jacob had to shoot better than three of his competitors. But a calm had settled over him and he was very confident.

For the third time he stepped to the fence. As he reloaded he heard his master call out. "Ah've another pound that says my boy'll win the turkey. Be there any takers?"

There was again a rush by men to place their money opposing him. Not one bet joined his.

"Yeh'll lose tha' pound," Jacob heard a man say with confidence, "even if yeh win the former, which I doubt. Do yeh not see Johannes Feeck's shootin'? He aint lost a match in a year an' a half."

Many other men agreed with him, and Jacob saw several of the shooters at the rail also nod. He already knew who Johannes Feeck was; all of his shots had been excellent.

He allowed the other four men to shoot. By now the others knew he preferred to shoot last but, as the youngest shooter, they obliged him. Three of the shots were exceedingly good and both of the bets against his master multiplied. Jacob knew his shot would have to be very very good, and he made it his best.

He shot half an inch. The third best had been five eights. He was in the final round. But Johannes' shot had been only three eights.

He feared his master would lose his last bet; but, to his shocked amazement, he watched his master calmly sweep up his prior winnings and place them all upon his final note. There was a frantic rush to add to the piles facing it. Jacob had never seen so much money in one place in his life.

The call came to reload. Jacob's hand shook as he did so. He had never loaded a gun so carefully before in his life. When it came time to insert the ball, he sorted through his bag rejecting three before he settled upon one which had no discernible mark upon its surface.

He glanced over at Johannes.

"Would yeh have me shoot first?" the man asked.

Jacob nodded.

When the man shot, Jacob could see he had made another excellent shot. For a moment he despaired; what chance did he have of besting it?

He lifted his rifle to his shoulder and settled his cheek against it. Now that the moment had come, he was again calm.

He sighted in upon his X, but then lowered his rifle to wipe his eyes.

The field was silent.

Once more he hoisted the rifle, sighted it and, when his gut said fire, pulled the trigger.

It was a very good shot, perhaps good enough, but it was impossible to tell. He glanced over at Johannes to find him watching him.

The man nodded, and said, "Win or lose, yeh've shot well."

Jacob did not know what to say, so just nodded back.

The boy whose job it was to collect and return the boards had handed them to the judges, and they were poring over their measurements.

Jacob glanced at his master, and wondered how he would react if he had lost. But the smith just grinned at him; he seemed to still be enjoying himself.

The judges were ready. Johannes' square was held high. "Five eights o' n'inch," was the verdict. Then it was Jacob's square. "Three quarter o' n'inch."

Jacob had lost.

He found a hand thrust at him; it was Johannes.

"I look forward ta facin' yeh again." The man shook his hand, and grinned. "Yeh'll not deny me shall yeh?"

Jacob glanced at his master who was cheerfully watching the piles of money disappear from before him. "No," he assured Johannes, "We'll meet again." He was confident the smith would ensure a rematch.

"I am sorry," he told the smith when they were finally alone.

"Fer what?"

"Fer losing."

"Hells bells, lad, d'yeh think Ah'm gonna complain about a three quarter inch shot?"

"But," said Jacob, "yeh lost all that money."

"Ach," the smith waved it away. "T'was only money. Ah never bet what Ah can nae lose." He grinned down upon Jacob.

"Besides, Ah did nae lose as much as yeh may think. D'nae forget Ah won my first three wagers."

"But yeh put all yer winnings upon the last wager."

"Did Ah now?" When Jacob did not answer, he continued, "P'raps yeh only thought Ah did."

"Yeh did not?"

"Nay, Ah slipped out a pound, three." He nudged Jacob. "And d'yeh nae recall I slipped yeh a pocket o' coins?"

Jacob had forgotten, and when he emptied his pocket and added it up he found he had a pound, six pence.

"All things considered," concluded the smith placidly, "Ah'd say we broke even." He elbowed Jacob gently, and grinned. "There be a shoot Wednesday next. Yeh wanna go?"

"Aye," Jacob said.

11 Prince Philip

March, 1769

Jacob sat morosely watching Philip play with the Indian children and Mateo. Woosamequin had been right, in the four months he and his brother had been coming to watch the children they had quickly and easily learned their language; while far from fluent, they were already quite proficient.

But he had made little headway in understanding Philip; the boy seemed to dislike him, and Jacob did not know why. He finally decided to ask Woosamequin.

The old man sighed, and said, "It is not yer fault, Jacob, and sorry I am he continues to treat yeh so. I had hoped it would be otherwise. Sit, if yeh would."

Jacob took a seat upon a mat facing the old Indian. The man considered him quietly for several long moments, and then said, "Yeh must know, Jacob, Philip and the rest of us here in this village are among the last of a great and powerful people. The Wampanoags once lived north of here, along the coast of what is now Massachusetts, and we ruled a hundred miles or more of the coast and far into the interior." His eyes grew distant. "Our chiefs were wise and noble and our warriors were feared and respected by all men."

He returned to the present, and considered Jacob keenly. "Philip is descended from those chiefs and is very proud of his heritage."

Jacob nodded. "He should be," he whispered.

"Aye," agreed the old man. "He should be." He said nothing more for a moment, and seemed lost in his thoughts.

Jacob cleared his throat. "Yeh should have named him after one of his ancestors," he ventured. "I have always wondered why he has a white man's name."

"A white man's name!" Woosamequin fumed. For a moment he glared at Jacob, but then his face mellowed into a deep sadness. "Yeh say that only because yeh have never been told."

"I've never been told what?" Jacob asked carefully.

The old man raised his chin proudly. "Yeh've never been told of Prince Philip and his war."

"Prince Philip?" Jacob shook his head. "I have not. Please tell me."

The Indian smiled, and settled himself. "When the white man first came, they settled upon Wampanoag land. Philip, whose name was then Metacom, was a mere lad at that time. He thought his father, the chief of the Wampanoag, whose name by the way was Woosamequin," the old man grinned, and inclined his head regally, "would drive these foreign people out, but instead of driving them from Wampanoag lands, he welcomed them.

"'Metacom, my son,' his father explained to him, 'these new men could become valuable allies. Our people have lately suffered an epidemic which has decimated our numbers. We have vacant lands and many enemies who lust to take them from us. It is wise we grant some land to these people if they shall then help us defend our remaining territories.'

"Thus, the Wampanoag did all they could to assist the white men. And the white men certainly needed their aid for they nearly all died that first year even with it. But eventually the white invaders thrived and more white men poured into their settlements every year. The boy Metacom watched their swift growth with alarm. He spoke of his alarm with his older brother, Wamsutta.

"'The white men grow more numerous every year, and every year they ask for more land.'

158

"His brother agreed, but grinned, and said, 'Our alliance with them has made our father and our people very strong; our enemies flee before us. I am glad their numbers are increasing; their increase is our increase. The land we grant them we can spare; we gain nearly as much each year from our enemies.'

"'But,' demanded Metacom, 'How long shall it be before they think themselves strong enough to stop requesting, and begin demanding? How long until they stop being our allies, and become our enemies?'

"His brother scoffed at him. 'Relations between us and them remain very friendly; the alliance is mutually beneficial.' He smiled condescendingly, and patted him on the head. 'Trust me; our father is far too wise to allow anything like you imagine to happen.'

"Metacom hated when his brother patted him on the head like he was a child, but he revered his older brother; if he said there was nothing to worry about, Metacom believed him. Besides, Wamsutta was right, their father was wise, and he was continuing to pursue friendly relations with the whites.

"In fact, to honor the white allies, Woosamequin, whom the whites referred to as Massasoit, had allowed the white leaders to rename his two sons. Thus Metacom had become named Philip while his older brother, Wamsutta, had become Alexander.

"Metacom, now Philip, decided his fears were groundless, and relaxed.

"The peaceful relations between the Wampanoag and the white invaders held so long as Woosamequin lived. When he died, Alexander became the new chief and the white men sent a messenger asking him to appear before their governors. Alexander expected no ill treatment, and went to them with only a few men.

"However, instead of recognizing him as their sovereign, as they had once recognized Massasoit, or even as an ally, the white men treated him as a subordinate. They demanded he swear his allegiance to their king.

"'I am the chief of the Wampanoag,' Alexander told them. 'How can a man who has never been to our lands and has never fought us much less conquered us be our ruler?'

"But he was told if he did not swear allegiance to their king, he would be imprisoned in a dungeon until he did. Alexander knew he could not resist them with the few men he had brought with him and, as a man of the open free forest, was terrified of confinement. He swore his allegiance, and was allowed to return to his people.

"But he was never again the same. He was unable to eat, he was unable to sleep, he was unable to carry out his duties. Within a month he was dead. The shame of what he had done had killed him.

"Philip became the new chief. He considered the white men to have killed his brother whom he had idolized and adored just as surely as if they had plunged a lance into his heart. His old fears now seemed confirmed, and to them was added an implacable hatred. Nonetheless, he tried to maintain peace and an alliance with the white men; it was still to the Wampanoag interest, but he never accepted their sovereignty over him or his people.

"For thirteen years he maintained the peace despite the increasingly insulting behavior of the whites toward him and the Wampanoag. But then a Wampanoag who the whites called John Sassamon was found murdered in a pond near Plymouth. This John Sassamon had been educated by missionaries, and had studied at Harvard.'"

"Studied at Harvard?" Jacob burst out. He clasped his hand over his mouth. "I'm sorry, I did not mean to interrupt yer story. But . . . the Indian had studied at Harvard?"

Woosamequin chuckled. "Yeh are surprised an Indian studied at Harvard? Yeh should not. There have been quite a number of us. I myself have studied there."

"Yeh . . . ?" Jacob had trouble getting his mind around the statement. "But then . . . why are yeh . . . ?"

"Why am I living in a cabin as a poor and common man?"

Jacob nodded mutely.

"Because it is here I belong. I did not go to Harvard to abandon my people; I went to better serve them. Here, among them, as one of them, I can best do so."

Jacob again nodded.

"Now, where was I? Oh yes, John Sassamon." The old Indian settled himself more comfortably. "The whites, you see, had come to think of John as almost a white man although he had never indicated any desire to be anything other than a Wampanoag. They presumed to arrest some Wampanoag men, try them for John's murder, and hang them.

"That action ended Philip's patience. All of the men involved had been Wampanoag; it had been his duty and right alone to address the murder, and bring the guilty to justice. Insults of great magnitude he had tolerated, but he could not tolerate their presuming to kill his subjects. He believed he owed his people his protection.

"He began to prepare for war.

"But he knew he could not only attack the white men living in his lands; by then there were many settlements of white men all up and down the coast. These other settlements would send men to aid those in Wampanoag lands. However, he reasoned the Indian tribes living beside those settlements were as angry as he.

"So he sent messengers to those tribes, many of whom were the Wampanoag ancient enemies, urging them join him in a great alliance to drive the white men from all of the lands. It took a great deal of negotiating and persuading, but the alliance was formed, and the war was begun.

"If the alliance had held, the white men would not now be in America; they would have been driven into the sea and every remnant would have died. But . . ."

Woosamequin's eyes were very sorrowful. "As soon as it became clear victory was within the grasp of the alliance, it was destroyed by tribes who sought to gain their own advantages over the others. And once the tribes became divided, the whites were able to concentrate upon one tribe at a time, and subdue them. Some of the tribes even turned against their former allies, and aided the white men for promised advantages. Only a few tribes remained faithful to Philip. They all suffered the fate of the Wampanoag."

Woosamequin looked Jacob in the eye. "In the end, it was other Indians who destroyed the Wampanoags, another Indian who shot and killed Philip. His head was severed from his body, carried back to Plymouth, and stuck upon a pole where it remained for twenty five years."

The man sat silent, and Jacob feared breaking it. Finally Woosamequin looked up, and said, "The white men do not like to remember how close they came to being defeated, and the Indian tribes who remain do not like to remember their treachery, so Philip is remembered by only the Wampanoags and the few other tribes which had remained faithful; all of whom are also now mere remnants. That is why yeh have never heard of Philip and his war."

Woosamequin smiled. "But that is who Philip is named after, not a white man. He has been taught to honor, and take pride in his namesake. Unfortunately his pride has become rancid from living as a member of a small, and often despised group." The old Indian looked Jacob in the eye. "Many white men treat us despicably, as if we are hardly human. Philip has experienced this, and his pride has made him rebel against it; to assume all white men think of him so."

"I do not think of him so," Jacob protested.

"I know yeh do not," Woosamequin said. "I knew that when yeh first came to me." He leaned forward. "But Philip does not. When he looks at yeh, he sees only a white man, and assumes yeh despise him. He trains with yeh only because I command him to." He grinned. "And because he is fond of Hannah."

"Why does he not see a white woman when he looks at her?"

"Because she has succeeded in destroying his prejudice against her. He knows she does not despise him." Woosamequin pursed his lips. "Yeh must do the same. But I am confident yeh shall do so." He leaned forward, and put his hand upon Jacob's shoulder. "Yeh must do so. That was why I chose to teach yeh and yer friends; because Philip's hatred and bias must be destroyed. I knew yeh could do so."

"Why me?"

"Because yeh have known prejudice as well, have yeh not?"

Yes, Jacob had. As a Jew he had known he was a despised minority. He was sure the only reason he was mostly free of the bias now was because Mr. Sablonski had chosen his associates with great care. But he wondered how Woosamequin had known.

The old Indian nodded his head. "Prejudice experienced leaves a mark upon a man. I knew yeh had experienced it, and I knew that experience would enable yeh to understand Philip and break through his bias." He sighed. "For his prejudice against the white men is as real as theirs against him."

Jacob nodded. "Why do yeh not hate the white man?" he asked. "After all they have done to yeh and yer people?"

Woosamequin smiled a sad smile. "None of the white men who humiliated and killed my people are now alive. None of the white men now alive are to blame for what their ancestors did. Besides, their ancestors only did what my ancestors would have done had they been able." He again put his hand upon Jacob's shoulder, and said, "Never hate another man for doing what yeh would do if yeh were in their shoes." He stood. "Yeh and yer brother had best hurry if yeh're to make it to Hannah's house before her."

He was right; Jacob called his brother, and ran.

12 Harvesting Saffron

June, 1769

Jacob gazed down the row of saffron plants stretching before him. It seemed every one of them was covered in blossoms. They all had to be stripped before nightfall.

Why do the Schwenkfelders grow such a demanding plant?

Although it was fortunate they did. Since the saffron plants had to be harvested the same day a flower opened and they all bloomed within a few weeks of each other, the Schwenkfelders were always eager to hire help and paid well. Mr. Wallace had released Jacob to earn what he could.

Jacob did not like harvesting saffron; it was tedious work, and his fingers were not nimble enough. The flowers themselves were not picked; that would have been easy. No. The Schwenkfelders harvested only the three stigmas and style of each flower which had to be carefully plucked and placed gently into the bag at his side.

But Jacob wanted to earn cash money quickly, and the saffron fields were the place to do it. He wanted a rifle.

He was nearly sixteen; the smith had agreed it was time he had his own rifle; had offered to sell him any rifle in his stock. But Jacob wanted to design, and build a rifle of his own. After expressing some reservations concerning his readiness for such a task, the smith had good naturedly agreed to allow him to try.

It is not like I shall not have him to advise and assist me; if my skills prove inadequate, I am sure he can set my errors right.

However, the materials for a good rifle were not cheaply gained, and he wanted only the very best. His master had offered him free use of any metal in his stock, but that Jacob had refused. He did not want to feel beholding.

He hefted his bag; it was only a quarter filled. It took a long time to fill a bag. But a full bag was exceedingly valuable; an ounce of saffron was worth an ounce of gold. Thus the excellent wages the Schwenkfelders were willing to pay.

Spending each weekend immersing himself in the Indian culture had caused Jacob to look at the Schwenkfelders and Amish in a new light; as an objective outsider, and the more he had done so the more he had found them both mystifying but fascinating. Both groups considered themselves to be Christian yet, unlike Christians Jacob had known previously, refused to take oaths, go to war, or establish an organized church organization. They also both refused to baptize their children, insisting baptism was for adults only. In these ways they were very distinct from most Christians and similar to each other. Jacob was sure that was a prime reason the Schwenkfelders had chosen to settle in Birdsboro and why the Amish had welcomed them; the Schwenkfelders were rather recent immigrants.

However in other ways the two groups differed significantly. For instance, the Schwenkfelders practiced the holy days of the Eastern Church religiously while the Amish observed the holy days of the Western Church casually. Before he had come to Birdsboro Jacob had never known there was an eastern and western division of Christians let alone that holy days was one of the main divisions between them.

He felt the division was foolish, for both claimed to follow the same scriptures; did not their scriptures determine their holy days? And the only holy days Jacob had been able to find in their scriptures were the same as in his own; the holy ordinances God had ordained for the Jews as eternal feasts. Yet these neither the Amish nor Schwenkfelders observed.

He had tried to convince the Gerbers to join him in his celebrations. It was hard to properly celebrate a holy day alone. After all, their Bible contained all of the Books of Moses as well as most of the other Jewish scriptures. He had shown them where their own scriptures clearly said these were God's ordnances which were to be practiced forever, but it had made no difference; they had refused to join him. It was not their tradition to practice the ordnances.

It is very strange. Christians all claim to follow the scriptures but have different traditions from each other. And their traditions are held more stringently than is the scripture.

One of the few nice things about reaping saffron was that many of the Amish and Schwenkfelders labored beside him and, to pass the time, were willing to answer his questions. Jacob was fortunate that day to have Levi Gnagi, the Amish bishop, reaping the row to his left. He turned to him, and pointed out the paradox he perceived.

The bishop listened quietly, and even agreed with him; up to a point. But then he eyed Jacob sadly, and said, "Unfortunately Jacob, it is the Jews; yourself included, who are truly bound by traditions. While I was in the old country I had many Jewish friends. I tried to show them where their traditions conflicted with their own scriptures, but they always refused to see it." He sighed. "Their traditions were more important."

Jacob began to object, but Levi asked, "Did you not tell me the rabbis taught God would not hold a slave responsible for breaking the law while he was in bondage?"

Jacob nodded.

The old Amishman shook his head. "Where in the Books of Moses does it say that?"

Jacob knew the answer. "It is written that masters are required to ensure their servants keep the Sabbath," he said. "Thus a master who does not is guilty."

"But where does it teach the slave is innocent?"

"Where does it teach he is not?"

"Nowhere within the five Books that I know," admitted Levi, "but the example of Daniel and his friends when they were ordered by the king to eat unclean foods does."

Jacob did not know how to refute that argument and it shook him to the core. Could it be the Rabbi's teaching had been false?

He did not want to even think about that possibility. He decided to think about it later.

He checked his bag again. It did not seem any fuller than it had been. *Lands, I hate picking saffron.*

But the bishop was not done with him. "Jacob," he asked, "will you at least consider that Jesus of Nazareth was the messiah; even though that means your ancestors have been mistaken?" He held out his hand. "If you will only consider the possibility, I shall consider the possibility we have been wrong to not celebrate the high Jewish feasts. Is it a deal?"

Jacob thought about it. Accepting that the Christians were right about Jesus felt like denying all he had been taught, negating all his ancestors had suffered, lived, and died for. But . . . considering the possibility . . . would that be denying them? His rabbi had taught him he should test all doctrines against the Books of Moses; would this not be what he was doing?

For the first time he felt himself objectively evaluating the Jews as he had the Indians and Amish. Could it be that much of what he had believed to be holy duty was in fact only cultural?

"You would have to prove it from the Books of Moses," he said.

"No," said Levi. "I shall not argue the case with you. I only ask you read with an open mind the four gospels relating the life of the Lord, beginning with the book of John. You, by yourself, shall judge if He qualifies as the messiah promised in the Books of Moses. In return, I shall agree to allow you to instruct me on the high feasts of the Jews. and promise I and my family shall celebrate them with you for one year." He again held out his hand. "Is it a deal?"

Jacob had been considering reading the stories of Jesus anyway; he wanted to learn for himself what the Christians believed, so he took the bishop's hand and shook it.

He stood straight, rubbed his aching back, and missed Hannah. He looked back, and found her scowling at him a good ten feet behind. He grinned apologetically, and began to collect from her row. He was rewarded by the quick flash of a smile as she began to collect as fast as she could.

He was sorry he had forgotten to help her. She had come all the way to the Schwenkfelder settlement to pick saffron with him, for him; she was giving all her earnings to him to help make his rifle. Since he was faster than she, she needed him to collect just a few from her row so they could keep together. Although with her nimble fingers he was sure she would actually be much faster than he if she were not such a perfectionist; she checked each blossom at least three times to be certain she had not missed the tiniest fragment.

She soon caught up, and they continued together without a word. It was one of the things he liked best about Hannah; she didn't need to talk all the time like most girls. She and he seemed able to understand each other, and enjoy each other's company without talking.

13 Hannah's Bear

April, 1770

Jacob loped quietly through the forest, his ears alert, and his eyes darting. He, Hannah, and Philip were chasing Mateo. He was quite sure they had him cornered in the small canyon before them, but he knew from experience how cunning his brother could be. After a year of Woosamequin's training, the time was long past when his brother could be tracked by the behavior of the birds. Woosamequin had taught them how to avoid disturbing them. And he had trained them to observe the animals around them; learn their tricks, especially those of the masked one of the forest, the raccoon. Even yet, Jacob knew, that varmint had tricks to teach them, but his brother knew many of them very well.

It was the general consensus that Matt was the most adept at avoiding capture, in part because he was so strong and agile as well as wily. One of his favorite tricks was to lay a short false trail only to backtrack, spring to a low hanging branch of a tree, and then descend from the tree, sometimes even crossing to an intertwining tree, to start a new trail many yards away.

However, Woosamequin had also taught them a great many tricks to tracking; things Jacob would never have noticed before they had begun their training now seemed obvious and easily discerned, and the rest had conceded he was the best tracker. He knew Mateo had passed this way, and had not returned.

He had sent Hannah to flank him a hundred yards to his left while Philip covered his right. He expected if his brother were to try to flank them, he would do so upon his right, and Philip's expertise was in spotting movement. They had all learned if Philip were close, their only option was to freeze; the slightest movement he would detect.

Hannah's forte was her intuition, but it was in some ways the most formidable. Whenever a trail was lost, the boys would look to her; she would guess where their prey had gone, plunge into the brush and, more often than not, regain the trail. Jacob had no idea how she did it.

He peered to his right, and caught a glimpse of Philip prowling through the forest with his fire hardened lance at the ready. He could easily imagine the boy's ancestors doing the same, and a chill ran down his back. Philip never went anywhere without his lance, even though there were no enemies in these woods.

Once Jacob had understood the reason for Philip's scorn for him, he had begun to understand and empathize with him. Even then it had taken him awhile to realize that Philip's attitude was justified, and that it was Jacob's fault.

He had thought that, because he did not despise the Indians or Philip but on the contrary esteemed them, he was not biased, and Philip had no cause to be prejudiced against him. But then he had realized he esteemed him, and the other Indians, only because they were Indian, and that doing so was as prejudicial as despising them only because they were Indian.

But, he had consoled himself, *it is not an offensive bias, why should Philip take offense?* But upon putting himself into Philip's moccasins and considering the matter, he had realized it was no less dehumanizing than any other bias. Philip was right to despise him and treat him as a white man instead of seeing him as a person because Jacob had never seen him as a boy; only as an Indian.

That was why Philip had always liked Hannah, Jacob had realized, because Hannah had always treated him as a person, not as an Indian.

Once he had started doing so, Philip had begun treating him as a person instead of a white man and the two had become, if not good friends, at least congenial companions.

There came the angry growl of a bear to his left followed by the crashing of underbrush. *Hannah!* He sprinted to his left, and found them in a small clearing; Hannah curled into a tight ball with the bear snuffling over her.

Good, she's remembered Woosamequin's advice. He had taught them a good defense against a bear is to play dead; often a bear shall then lose interest and leave. But he had also told them it was not a certain defense; on occasion a bear would maul a body.

Jacob saw a tiny tremble run down the girl's arm. The bear saw it too; quicker than thought he slapped her across the clearing as easily as Jacob might have slapped a rat. Four ugly red streaks appeared on Hannah's back; she writhed in the air, and screamed.

The bear reared upon his hind legs, roared, and charged, but his roar was joined by another; one Jacob dimly realized came from his own throat. He was hurtling toward the bear with his knife in his hand. He intercepted it several yards from Hannah, and leaped upon its back.

There was a frenzy of activity, but he clung tenaciously, and plunged his knife into the bear. He could not allow himself to be thrown from his back; only there was he somewhat protected from the horrid claws and fangs. The bear reared, Jacob pulled himself up higher, and plunged his knife into its neck; he had to find the jugular, only by doing so could he hope to end the conflict.

But the bear continued his motion to fall backward upon him. Only at the last moment did Jacob realize his intent, and thrust himself aside. He landed hard in the sod, with the bear crashing beside him, and rolled frantically, expecting to feel the three inch claws rake him at any instant.

The bear rose to its feet, and roared but, instead of pouncing upon Jacob, spun away. Jacob heard a sharp crack, saw

Philip fly through the air, and realized the boy had plunged his wooden lance into the bear's far side. But he also saw the bear had exposed its throat. He leaped to his feet, plunged his knife into it, and sliced a long gash. To his relief, a geyser of blood spurted forth, the bear turned, groaned, staggered, and collapsed.

Jacob glanced to where Philip was rising from the brush where he had flown; he seemed unhurt. "Get yer grandpa," he ordered, and the boy ran. Jacob turned his attention to where Hannah lay; he was afraid of what he would see.

He found her staring at him with shining eyes. She was not crying but, for the first time since he had met her, seemed helpless. She mutely held out her arms to him; he ran over, dropped to his knees, and held her, being careful not to hurt her wounded back. She snuggled into his arms, buried her face into his shoulder, and the tears came. She had as yet said not a word.

"Be yeh all right?" he whispered.

She nodded, but cried harder.

She was not all right he knew. Not only was her back laid open, but her left leg was twisted oddly and already turning a horrid shade of purple. It was broken.

He did not know what to do, and only held her as gently as he could, and allowed her to cry. Emotions he had not known he had surged through him, and he realized how very fond he was of her. She was not just a girl; she was not just a friend; she was Hannah, and he didn't want to lose her.

He became aware of Mateo's ashen face beside him, and soon Philip came running with Woosamequin and two of his daughters close behind. The old Indian took Hannah gently from him and, seeing her wounded back, unceremoniously ripped the top half of her dress from her.

Jacob looked away embarrassed. He had never seen a girl half naked before. He saw Mateo watching entranced, and told him to turn around also. He did not wish to shame Hannah. But he could not erase the memory of the brief glimpse he had had from his mind. Despite the cruel gashes upon her back, Hannah's body was . . . very comely. He led the two boys to the edge of the clearing. Woosamequin and the two women were attending to the girl's wounds; it was best, he thought, to stay out of their way.

It was not long before the old Indian came to them; with a few curt phrases he sent Philip racing back to the camp for some items and, giving his tomahawk to Jacob, ordered Mateo and him to fetch a generous supply of vines.

The two brothers did not ask why, only hurried to obey. It felt good to be doing something even if they did not know why the vines were needed.

When they returned, they found Hannah with her leg splinted and her back wrapped with bandages which had been smeared with some foul smelling ointment. The bottom half of her dress was secured by a leather string tied about her waist but, despite the bandages, her upper half was still embarrassingly exposed.

When Hannah saw them, she dropped her eyes, and blushed bright red. It was the first time Jacob had ever seen her disconcerted and he did not like it, but he did not know how to change it.

But Mateo did. Stripping off his own shirt, he offered it to her.

Hannah took it gratefully but, when she tried to raise her arms to put it on, grimaced, and lowered them again. One of Woosamequin's daughters took the shirt from her and, with a gentleness that amazed Jacob, worked it carefully up her arms, and then, without raising her arms, slipped it over her head, and down over her body. The smile upon Hannah's face as it emerged from the shirt relieved Jacob. She was going to be all right.

Woosamequin took up an ax Philip had brought, dropped two saplings, and stripped them of branches. He then quickly and easily wove the vines the brothers had gathered into a long thin bier between them. He told Mateo to place one end upon his shoulders while Jacob held the other as level as he could. The Indian then fashioned a sling with more vines so that they went over Jacob's shoulders and supported the bier level without his having to hold it.

He then carefully lifted Hannah to lie upon her stomach, and ordered them to take her home. It was a load, but much easier than Jacob would have suspected. They were soon in sight of her house but, just before they arrived, he heard Hannah say, "I thank yeh for saving my life, Jacob."

"Ye're welcome, Hannah. T'was nothing. I'm just glad yeh be all right." He was again surprised by the depth of the emotions which surged through him; he was very very glad she was all right.

"It was not either nothing," Hannah retorted. "I shall never forget it."

There was a scream from the house; Hannah's sister, Rachel, had spotted them. Despite his worries for Hannah, Jacob grinned to himself wryly. *Too bad Sarah wasn't the first to see us, she would not have screamed.* Sarah, Hannah's other sister was much more like she herself, not as . . . well, not as girlish. But the scream had had its desired effect; the house spewed forth her family.

Jacob struggled to maintain his balance as Hannah rolled upon her side, held out her arms, and cried, "Mama!"

She was soon enveloped in her mother's arms, and both Jacob and Mateo staggered as she was, but Mr. O'Malley caught hold of the bier and steadied it. Mr. Wallace had appeared behind Jacob, and he felt him lift the burden from his shoulders. He remembered his master spent every Sunday with the O'Malleys.

For the second time Hannah was crying; this time freely, unabashedly, like a tiny child.

"Shh, my darling, yer mother is here. That's right, show me where it hurts. Yeh'll be all right. There's my brave gal."

Jacob was amazed; her mother was as calm and calming as if Hannah had merely fallen and scraped her knee, but he could see her already surveying her injuries.

"We must get her inside."

"Yes," her father agreed. He lifted the bier from Mateo's shoulders. "We'll take her, lads."

Mr. Wallace had already taken Jacob's end from him, and the boys watched as she was borne toward the house. Jacob was unsure what they should do, but Hannah glanced back at them, and cried, "Do not leave me," so he hurried to join them.

"What happened," her father demanded as they walked.

Jacob tried to explain as concisely as he could, but Hannah interrupted him. Her tale painted him so heroically, he felt himself blushing. The glance her father gave him he found hard to fathom. *Does he commend me or . . . blame me for not protecting her better?*

The two men carried her up the stairs to the second floor and down the hall to her room. Jacob stopped uncertainly in the hall; he was not sure he should enter a girl's bedroom, but her father called him in.

"Take my end so I may lift her into the bed."

Jacob did so, and then, with Mr. Wallace, laid the bier aside.

He glanced guiltily about the bedroom feeling he was invading Hannah's privacy, yet unable to resist. It was not at all as he had imagined a girl's bedroom to be; certainly not like the Gerber girls' half of the loft. For one thing, several square feet of her wall was covered by dried insects, each neatly pinned and labeled with a name.

Hannah saw him staring at them, and grinned. She was back to her old confident self and sitting up in her bed. "I like insects," she admitted. She held out her arms, and, despite his embarrassment, he went to her. Before her parents and everyone else, she pulled him down into an embrace, and whispered into his ear, "I love yeh, Jacob Schram. I have always loved yeh, and I always shall."

She released him, and he stood wondering how to respond. He wondered if the others in the room had heard her. He finally said only, "I hope yeh shall recover fully," turned upon his heel, and escaped.

As he and Mateo hiked back to the Gerbers, he wondered what it meant. Did Hannah really love him? He had never had anyone tell him they loved him; certainly not a girl. *She is only twelve,* he reminded himself. *She can't love me, it is a mere infatuation.* But . . . Hannah was not like other girls, and he remembered the smith's teasing of him; saying he had caught Hannah's eye. Could it have been more than teasing?

He felt again the surge of affection he had felt in the forest, but it was more than mere affection. Could it be that he . . . ?

No! He refused to believe it. *She is only twelve and I am only fifteen. We do not love each other; we merely like each other, we are friends. We have had an emotional experience together, of course it stirred our emotions, but that is all it be. It shall not last.*

But late that night, alone with the softly snoring Mateo, his arms remembered her snuggled within them . . . and he wanted to believe their love would last.

14 I love you too

May, 1770

It had been a month since Hannah had been attacked, and it appeared she would recover fully from her injuries. But she was of course unable to accompany Jacob and Mateo to visit the old Indian. Jacob had felt almost guilty going without her, but she had insisted he and Matt should go.

It was not the same; he missed her, and her absence made it even more clear how very fond he had become of her.

That Sunday just before it was time for them to go, Woosamequin presented the boys with the nicely tanned bearskin and bade them take it to Hannah.

Jacob was glad for an excuse to visit her for, although he had visited her several times, it being appropriate to visit an injured friend, even if that friend was a girl, he had been too embarrassed to go more often. He feared someone might think his visits portended more than mere friendship.

They met Hannah's father as he was coming from his barn. When they showed him the skin, he was very pleased. "Ye boys be certain to tell Woosamequin how thankful we be." His eyes misted. "This was exceedingly thoughtful of him."

Sarah, Hannah's little sister spotted them, and came running, calling for her mother and sister to come and see the lovely bear skin. She buried her face in the fur. "Oh, it's so soft!" She glanced up at her father with shining eyes. "How did they make it so soft?"

Her mother and sister had arrived. Mrs. O'Malley ran her hand over both the fur and skin sides. "They did an excellent job." Her eyes glowed. "Making it so soft required a good deal of labor for the old Indian and his daughters." She glanced up at her husband. "Perhaps . . . mayhap yeh are right; we should allow her to return to Woosemquin when she recovers."

Mr. O'Malley nodded. "It is a valuable gift; particularly since it is the skin of the beast which attacked her."

He glanced at Jacob; Jacob no longer had trouble reading it. Both he and Hannah's mother had thanked him repeatedly for saving their daughter; he was silently thanking him again.

Her father gathered the skin from the girls and his wife, folded it carefully, and handed it back to Jacob. "She is in the parlor where she can enjoy the sun. Yeh may take it to her."

"Yeh do not wish to take it to her?" Jacob asked surprised.

The man considered him, and slowly shook his head. "No. This bear's attack was something yeh boys and Hannah shared. Giving her its skin is something no one else should ointrude upon."

"Aw, Pa, can't we . . .," began Rachel, but she was silenced by a glance from her father. He turned back to Jacob, and pointed his chin. "Go."

Jacob and Mateo went but, when they reached the porch, Mateo glanced at Jacob slyly, and stopped. "The bear was dead when I arrived. Y.eh should take it to her alone."

Jacob was sure he would always remember the delight upon her face when Hannah saw the skin. She had never seemed so beautiful.

She had him spread it out upon the couch where she lay, and her hand immediately went to the knife hole in its back which Woosamequin had left open.

She looked up with shining eyes. "This is the wound yeh made that saved my life."

He squatted beside her, and also traced the cut with his finger, and she grasped his hand in hers. "I was so afraid yeh would be killed," he muttered.

"Yeh could have been killed trying to save me."

He looked into her face, and it seemed the most natural thing in the world to say, "Yer life means more to me than my own. I . . . I love you." And he knew that he did.

15 Father

November, 1770

At long last, Jacob's rifle was finally completed. It had been a long task, but a satisfying one.

"Try 'er out." he urged his brother.

"Be yeh sure?" Mateo hesitated although his eyes shone. "I would not . . . Yeh've only fired 'er a few times yerself."

"Here," Jacob laughed, thrusting his new rifle at his brother. "Shoot 'er a few times. I want yeh to."

He could tell his brother ached to do so, but still the boy stepped back, and stared up at Jacob. "What if I . . . Yeh've worked so hard . . ."

"Ye'll not," Jacob assured him. "An' ifin yeh do, I did a lousy job makin' 'er. Take 'er."

Mateo took the rifle eagerly, and ran his hand over the smooth barrel and stock lovingly. "She is a beautiful rifle, Jacob." He looked up with pride for his brother. "Yeh did a good job."

Jacob snorted. "I had a great deal of help." The sheen of the stock was due to Mateo himself; the Gerbers had told him of the many hours his brother had spent with a bit of glass smoothing it. Then, every night for a week, he had mixed soot and oil and rubbed it in until it was as dark and glossy as satin.

Also Jacob knew he could never have forged the metal parts had not it been for the hours Hannah had spent pumping the bellows, and handing him tools. And he could not count the times he had called upon Mr. Wallace for advice or assistance. It had been he who had effortlessly eliminated the tiny bow Jacob had striven for hours to rid from the barrel.

Yet it was his rifle, forged by his hand, and to his specifications. And she shot wonderfully; though it was Jacob's subjective opinion, he was convinced she fired more accurately than most.

Now he urged his brother to try his hand. Mateo was getting to be quite a good shot. *He'll soon be competing in shoots too.* He wondered what it would be like, competing against his own brother.

As his brother reloaded, Jacob saw Mr. Wallace coming, and went to meet him.

"Ah see yeh're shootin' er again," his master observed.

"Aye." Jacob grinned. "I must familiarize meself with 'er if I'm to shoot 'er next week."

"Aye, the shoot," the smith mused. He cocked his head, and asked, "D'yeh believe yeh'll be familiar enough with 'er to compete?"

"Aye," Jacob assured him. He did not say so, but he believed he could already shoot more accurately with his new rifle than he could with the smith's rifle.

"Aye." The smith sat himself upon a stump, again cocked his head, and considered Jacob for a long moment. Finally he asked, "Yeh've heard o' the match they've organized on the New Jersey side?"

"Aye," Jacob replied. Who had not heard of the meet? It was expected to draw a huge number of shooters. The top prize was a yoke of oxen.

"Ah've a mind ta enter yeh in it."

"Me? But . . . the best shooters within a hundred miles'll be there.

"Yeh are the best shot in a hundred miles," said Mateo who had stopped shooting, and come over to listen.

Jacob laughed at him. "I appreciate yer confidence, my brother, but I am not that good."

"He is that good, aint he, Mr. Wallace."

Mr. Wallace pursed his lips. "He may be; he may be nae. Th' only way we'll know is if he tries himself agin the others." He fixed his eye upon Jacob. "Be yeh willing to try?"

Did Jacob want to try himself against the best there was? Yes, he very much did. "But New Jersey is so far away."

"Long day's ride," the smith agreed. "A day long shoot, and then a day an' a half journey ta return."

"Why a day and a half to return?"

His master winked. "I expect the yoke o' oxen'll slow us a bit." He smiled at Jacob's face. "There are a dozen or so o' my mates as have agreed to go ifn we have yeh to represent us. It is time the rest o' the world knows o' us in Berks County." He arched an eyebrow. "Will yeh go? We'll pay yer entry fee, and arrange yer lodging."

Jacob glanced at Mateo; he could see he very much wanted to go also. "Can Matt come too?"

Mr. Wallace also glanced at the boy, and grinned. "Why not." He turned back to Jacob. "So yeh'll go?"

"Aye, and I thank yeh, sir."

The smith nodded, and rose to go.

But Jacob was thinking. "I would be allowed to keep any prize I may win, would I not?"

His master seated himself again. "Aye. Yeh always own what yeh win; we'd nae claim it." He grinned at Jacob. "Why? Are yeh desiring a yoke o' oxen?"

Jacob did not answer at once, but yes, he did desire the yoke. Could he but win it his plans would be advanced by nigh a year, mayhap more. "Aye," he finally admitted. "T'would be a great gain."

"T'would be," agreed the smith, "fer a man who had use fer 'em. Are yeh plannin' to have a use fer 'em?"

"Aye." Jacob was snatched back from the contemplation of what such a windfall could do for his prospects. He seated himself before his master. "I shall not be yer apprentice for much longer." He glanced at the smith. "Not that I find my estate irksome."

The smith nodded. "T'will be over soon, true enough--two years. Ah'll nae be lying when Ah say twill be hard ta see yeh go. Still, Ah can nae expect yeh to stay."

"There is not work enough fer the two o' us."

The smith nodded in agreement. "So yer makin' yer plans as a good laddie ought. Are yeh willin' to share 'em?"

"Aye," Jacob replied. "I value yer advice." The words came in a rush. "Yeh remember Ian McNitt's brother who visited him a month past? He has a place in the Kishacoquillas Valley northwest o' here. He claims the land there is the richest the Lord created, and settlers are arriving every year; there are nigh two hundred souls already. But there is not a smith."

His master grinned. "An' yeh intend to supply that lack."

"Aye. If I can get there before another." He glanced at the smith. "Do yeh think the plan viable? Ifn I win the yoke I'd be a long way towards settin' meself up on a farm. It'd save me most a year. Twixt the farm and smithin' fer the settlers, do yeh not think I could make a go o' it?"

The smith nodded soberly, and then smiled. "Aye. Tis a sound plan. A few lean years mayhap, but then yeh'll prosper. Twill be sad ta have yeh move so far away, but it be the thing ta do. The future for yeh is in the west." He glanced over at Mateo. "Matt'll go with yeh?"

"Aye."

"I expected as much." His master grinned. "Though yeh could leave 'im 'ere as me new apprentice." When Jacob shook his head, the grin grew larger. "An' unless I miss my guess, he is nae the only one yeh intend to accompany yeh."

Jacob stared at the ground. He felt his face grow hot. "Aye."

"Have yeh spoken to 'er o' yer plans?"

"Aye."

"Have yeh spoken to 'er father?"

"Nae," he muttered. He looked up at the smith. "It is at least two years in the future."

The smith chuckled, stood, and put a hand upon his shoulder. "I'd speak to him forthwith. He'll require the two years to adjust to the idea."

"Yeh do not think he'll accept me?"

"Ach, he'll accept yeh, no fear o' that; the man thinks the world o' yeh. But yeh're proposin' to take his daughter into the forest so far he may never see 'er again." He cleared his throat. "Speak to the man forthwith."

* * * *

Jacob sat across from Hannah's father, and outlined his plans for the future. He did his best to sound confident, and to paint his future as rosy as he could. "If I win the yoke o' oxen," he said, "I'll be well on my way to becomin' self sufficient. By the time my apprenticeship is over, in two years, I'll likely have secured the rest o' what I'd need to make the move."

Hannah's father nodded sagely. "It would seem yeh've thought yer future out very carefully and wisely."

"Aye, thank yeh sir. I've tried hard to." There was a silence. *This is the hard part. How does one ask a father to give you his daughter?*

"I desire . . . that is . . . I'll be asking yeh to allow me to take Hannah with me . . . as my wife."

The man before him did not reply, and the silence was heavy until Jacob asked, "Be that agreeable?"

Hannah's father still did not reply, but rose, opened a cabinet, and poured a small glass of rum for each of them. Handing one to Jacob, he settled himself in his chair, and regarded him for a moment. His eyes became distant. "Taint like I did not know this day'd come; I knew it the day she was born, but . . ." His eyes focused upon Jacob. "An' I've known the day was nigh for the past year or so. Still, I thought I'd have more time." Rising the glass to his lips, he gulped it down. "Yeh'll have yer own daughter some day, Jacob. Then yeh'll understand."

"T'will not be for two years at the least," Jacob offered.

Her father laughed. "Twill be a wrenching blow when it comes time for her to go with yeh," he admitted. "One I do not anticipate. But that is not what I am mournin' now."

"What then?"

"When I tell the world I've given her to yeh, she shall no longer be my little gal; she'll be yer intended. Yeh may think that a trivial distinction, but . . ." He paused. "It is very large."

Jacob did not know what to say. This was not at all what he had expected. "She shall always be yer daughter," he finally stated.

Her father smiled a sad smile. "Aye, that she shall." His smile grew into a real smile. "An' t'would be a lie if I denied I'll be proud to call yeh my son-in-law."

"So . . ." Jacob asked carefully, "I may have her?"

Her father considered him, and then he said, "Let's wait until we see if yeh win those oxen."

"If I do not, shall yer answer be no?" He was far from confident he could win them.

"No," her father laughed. He grew serious. "But it shall be 'wait'. Yeh must be able to support her before I'll grant yeh her."

Jacob nodded. It was now trebly important he win the upcoming shoot. "We'll be leaving Wednesday next and returning by Saturday."

Hannah's father nodded. "I'll be asking yeh to keep our conversation private, Jacob. Others should not know before it is announced to the families. O' course Matt is yer family so yeh may tell him. If yeh win, I'll ask yeh and him to join us for Sunday dinner. I'll make the announcement then. Are yeh agreed?"

"Aye."

Hannah's father returned to the cabinet. "Until Sunday next then." He refilled his glass, and turned to lift it toward Jacob. "Good luck to yeh . . . son."

Jacob took his still full glass, and touched it carefully against his. "Thank yeh . . . father."

It had been nearly a decade since he had called any man 'father'. It felt good.

16 Dave Elerson

December, 1770

Jacob watched as the shots continued to ring out. He did not like being in the midst of such an enormous crowd; three hundred shooters were competing, and each man seemed to have half a dozen men cheering him on. On every side raucous men were jostling him, and at the periphery were a score of wagons with women selling a variety of foods.

Mateo nudged him, and handed a sandwich containing a thick slab of some form of meat to him. Jacob took it gratefully, but gnawed at it without tasting it.

He had had the misfortune to be assigned to the second set of shooters. He had made what he had believed to be an excellent first shot; had beaten the four others of his group handily. But, as he had watched the shelves where the top boards were placed in the order of their accuracy, his board had been pushed further and further down the line. The shelves would only hold eighty one boards; if his was pushed off, he would not pass to the next round. He had less than ten remaining betwixt his board and that fate with sixty men left to shoot.

I must make my next shot a far better one, if I even get another. Only twenty seven shooters would be allowed to pass to the third round.

"Come on," Mateo urged. "Watching aint gonna change what shall be. Walk around with me until the first round is over."

Jacob allowed his brother to lead him away from the center of the shooting. He knew the boy was right; watching and worrying would change nothing.

That's the way Mateo is about everything. He never worries, just accepts whatever happens, and rolls with circumstances, be they good or bad.

He wished he could be more like him.

Then the horn was blown indicating the end of the first round of shooting, and he and his brother hurried back to see if he was still alive.

He was, and he went forward with the other shooters to draw for his group for round two. He was pleased to find he drew group fifteen; very near the end. The man who had shot the best shot of round one, a rangy Virginian named Dave Elerson, advanced automatically to round three, which left eighty men; sixteen groups of five to shoot.

Jacob stared at the Virginian. He was not envious exactly, but he did wonder how it felt to have bested all three hundred men who had shot. And he did envy him a little for being able to sit out the next round.

Still, he thought, *he may not be the one to win. It could be that his first shot was an exceptionally lucky one.*

But the longer he gazed at the man, the less he believed it; Dave Elerson carried himself with an easy relaxed air of confidence and competence.

With a start, Jacob realized the Virginian was regarding him back; he had caught him staring at him. Jacob's first impulse was to blush, and look away in confusion, but he forced himself to hold the man's gaze.

To his surprise, Dave suddenly grinned widely, doffed his coon-skin cap, and nodded. Jacob grinned, and nodded back. He realized he liked this Dave Elerson.

Mateo tried to persuade Jacob to take another walk instead of watching the first fourteen groups shoot, but he refused; he wanted to see who he would be shooting against. Besides, he enjoyed watching the shoot now; somehow the fact that his shot was yet to come removed his fear; regardless of how well the others shot, he would have a chance to better them.

Finally it was time for his group, and Jacob stepped to the rail, and began to load his rifle. The shelf was filled with twenty six exceptional shots; he knew that he would have to make an exceptional shot himself if he was to bump any of them to earn a place in round three.

He had made shots equal to them in former shoots, but not consistently. He ran over everything the smith had taught him, and took his aim. One of the things the smith had taught him was to trust his instincts; to squeeze off his shot when his gut told him.

"If yeh d'na shoot until yer mind tells yeh yer aim is true," he had said, "yeh'll over analyze it, and foul yer shot every time."

Jacob's gut said his aim was true, and he squeezed the trigger.

With a mixture of delight and despair he watched his board placed in the number nineteen spot, moving all to the left of it over a space, dropping the leftmost off the shelf. He was delighted, because he was still alive for round three, but he despaired because he knew he had made the best shot he was capable of making, yet eighteen men had out-shot him. Somehow he would have to do better.

But how could he do better than his best?

Mateo understood and participated in his delight, but did not understand his despair.

"Yeh knew there would be very good shots here," he said. "No one shall think less o' yeh if yeh are not the best."

"But the oxen," Jacob said despondently. "I came to win the oxen."

"Three hundred men came to win the oxen," his brother sniffed. "Only one'll win 'em. T'will be who it will be."

"But . . ." Jacob had already told Mateo what was riding on winning these oxen.

"Mr. O'Malley shall give you Hannah," Mateo said patiently in German in case any were listening. "He as much as said he would. Be it this Sunday, or a year from now, or five years from now, he shall give her to you. Winning or not winning today shall not change that."

And just like that, Jacob's entire view of the day changed. He did not have to win. Certainly he desired to win; it would be gloriously wonderful if he did win, but he did not have to win.

He grinned down upon his brother. "Yeh always see the bright side o' things don't yeh?'

His brother shrugged. "I only see things as they be."

The horn sounded. It was time again to draw for a group. There were five groups of five; only seven men would survive to round four. The two best shots of round two advanced automatically. Jacob drew the first group.

He stepped to the rail confidently. Now that it no longer mattered if he won or lost, he could enjoy the experience. Still, he reloaded with extreme care. He still desired to win; unlikely though he knew his chances were. He settled his rifle against his shoulder, and caressed it with his cheek.

But he then remembered something old Woosamequin had told him; that wetting the far sight of a rifle helped one to focus and aim. He decided he would try it. He lowered his rifle, self consciously licked his fingers, and wet the tip of the far sight. He knew hundreds of men were watching him, but he knew most would attribute it to a quirk of superstition.

He again settled his rifle, and sighted it in. To his amazed delight he saw the old Indian had been right; the bit of spit on the sight caused it to shine just enough to make it stand out in bold relief. His gut told him he was dead on aim and, without a conscious decision, the trigger was squeezed, and the rifle fired. Jacob knew immediately he had made an excellent shot. Indeed, when the round was done, Jacob's board stood proudly at number three.

But, he reminded himself, only three men would survive round four.

Again he drew the first group of five; again he wet his sight and then took his very best shot; again his was the third best. He was in the final round. He felt giddy, almost slap happy.

He looked at the two men who were his competitors. One was a burly bearded man who had amazed Jacob with his skillful shooting; for some unreasoned prejudice, Jacob had assumed accurate marksmen to be thin, but watching this man shoot had put the lie to it. Jacob was surprised to realize he had not as yet caught the man's name.

The other contender was the rangy Virginian, Dave Elerson, who had won the first round. Jacob caught him glancing at him with a grin, and he grinned, and nodded back. He was glad Dave was in the final too, he liked him.

The best shot of the final round would win the match and the yoke of oxen. The second best would win a voucher for a custom made Golcher rifle. Had Jacob not just made his own rifle he may have lusted for that. The worst of the third would still win fifteen dollars which to Jacob was a sizable sum. He realized with awe one of these prizes were guaranteed him.

Still, there was only one he truly desired.

He glanced again at Dave; and his heart quailed; how could he hope to win against him? The Virginian had not only bested the field the first round, but the third round as well. He had only shot twice in the entire competition, and both times had shot the most accurately.

Jacob drew the second shot; the burly man was first, and Dave was to shoot last. Jacob wished he could shoot after Dave; then he would have a goal to surpass, even if it would likely be a very difficult one. As it was, he feared that no matter how well he shot, the Virginian would better him. But, he had to accept what was.

He was vaguely aware there was noise and turmoil all around him, but heard none of it as he stepped to the rail for his final shot. Very carefully he reloaded, wet his sight, and drew his aim. He was pleased to see his shot was judged better than the burly man who had shot before him but, as he had feared, when Dave shot last, it was judged the best.

Jacob had come in second, and had won the Golcher rifle. He went to congratulate Dave, and to tell him he had deserved to win, as indeed he had. To his surprise however, he found the man cussing himself under his breath. When Dave realized Jacob had heard him, he grinned sheepishly, and said, "I should'a shot wide. I meant to."

"Yeh meant to lose?" Jacob asked.

"I meant to come in second," the Virginian said. "I came here to win the voucher for the Golcher rifle. Mr. Golcher makes the finest rifles in the world. Now I'll have to try to sell the yoke to raise enough money to pay him to make me a rifle; assuming I can get him to take me on. I hear he's booked solid for most o' the year."

"I came to win the yoke," said Jacob. "But I have the voucher. Are yeh a mind to trade?"

The rangy Virginian seemed to be considering accepting the trade, but the crowd had heard their exchange, and the cry went up for a shoot off.

Dave grinned at their demands, and he held out his hand to Jacob. "What do yeh say, shall we shoot for it? Winner takes both?"

Jacob's inclination was to refuse. Better a valuable voucher than nothing at all, and Dave had proven a formidable foe. But he saw his brother in the crowd urging him to accept, and thought, *Why not; at the least it'll be fun. Besides, it'll give my master opportunity to bet big.* His master had promised him ten percent of all his winnings. So he took the hand, and shook it to the resounding roar of approval from the crowd.

"Instead of riding it all upon one shot," suggested Dave, "what say we shoot a triangle?"

"What is a triangle?" asked Jacob.

"We each shoot three shots at one board," said Dave, "then a straight peg shall be placed in each hole, a string stretched around them, and the shortest string shall win."

Jacob nodded. "Let's move the distance to fifty paces," he suggested. He hoped to improve his odds. He had learned his accuracy did not fade as quickly with distance as most of his opponents. He hoped this would prove true with Dave as well.

The Virginian nodded his acceptance. "Do yeh wish to shoot first or last?"

"Last," Jacob replied. He always preferred to have a goal to surpass.

Two boards each a foot square were procured and one was placed at fifty paces. Dave slowly and carefully loaded and shot three times. After the second and third shot a boy who stood near the target called out its distance from the first. His board was retrieved, the pegs were placed, and the string drawn. The judges proclaimed it was exactly eight inches.

The crowd was impressed, and the betting, which had already favored the Virginian turned markedly against Jacob. But Jacob had learned from former shoots not to be dismayed by having the odds be against him.

"It only increases our opportunity for profit," the smith would say.

Besides, he was very pleased with his opponent's shots; he had been correct; the added distance had greatly decreased the Virginian's accuracy. His eyes were not so sharp at a distance as Jacob was confident his own were. He believed he could now beat the man fair and square.

His board was placed, and Jacob loaded, and fired.

"Dead center," called the boy. The crowd cheered, but Jacob knew it meant nothing. The only thing that mattered was how close his next two shots were to the first.

Again he loaded, and aimed. But, just as his gut said 'dead on', and he began to squeeze the trigger, his back received a cruel blow which threw his shot down. He had been hit by a stone.

He spun around to find the source of the rock, but found Mateo already on top of a man much his superior in size and weight. But the ferocity of the boy's attack was overwhelming that advantage.

Trust Mateo to have been covering my back, but should not someone break up the fight?

He considered doing so himself, but saw the crowd was avidly watching, and bets were flying. It was not until the man produced a knife that they were forced apart.

Jacob went, and inspected his brother. The lobe of his left ear was dangling from where his opponent had tried to bite it off, and, when Mateo smiled, his teeth were red with blood. At first Jacob thought he had lost some teeth, but soon learned the blood was mostly the man's. Mateo had bitten also. In fact it had been the wound he had inflicted upon his foe's shoulder that had caused him to draw the knife.

The man was escorted from the crowd, and attention reverted to Jacob. Jacob's supporters were clamoring for him to be allowed to make a new second shot, but the judges, after consulting among themselves, disagreed. The shot would stand.

The boy called it had hit three inches and a bit to the right of his first. It was nigh impossible to win now; Jacob would have to place his third shot almost exactly betwixt the first two. His length around the two was already six inches; he could only gain two. But he had no choice but to make the best of the deal. For the last time of the day, he reloaded, drew his bead, and fired.

"Miss," the spotter cried. A groan went up from the crowd, but the boy yelled again, "Clean miss." He grabbed the board from the rail, and ran it to the judges.

The crowd parted to allow Jacob to pass to the judge's bench. He could not believe he had missed the board completely, but there were indeed only two holes. For a moment he wondered if, in the confusion, he had neglected to load a bullet. He did not believe he could have done so. But neither could he believe he had missed the board completely.

Dave Elerson did not believe he had missed either. He demanded to see the board. But he did not even glance at the front; instead he turned it over. He nudged Jacob, and pointed to a marked bulge in the back. With a grin he pulled his knife, and began to pry the wood apart.

In short order he produced a misshapen bit of lead. He kept digging and soon produced a second. He held them up to the judges and the crowd.

"He shot his third bullet down his first bullet's hole. I have only seen it happen once before; now I've seen it again."

One of the judges grabbed the board, and thrust his little finger down the second hole. The expression upon his face told everyone he had encountered the third bullet. They had to measure Jacob's string around only the two pegs. It was judged to be five and three quarter inches long.

A hand slapped Jacob hard upon the back, and a second grabbed his right hand and shook it. Both hands belonged to the Virginian. "Dem fine shootin'."

"But," said Jacob, "yeh could have kept outa it. No one would have known, and yeh'd have won."

Dave shook his head. "I do not take what does not belong to me. Yeh beat me fair and square. I'd have it no other way." He grinned sheepishly. "Though losin' that Golcher rifle did tempt me for a moment."

"Yeh can have the rifle," Jacob said. "I told yeh I have no use for it."

But the tall Virginian again shook his head. "I told yeh I do not take what is not mine. Yeh won it, and it is yern."

"It is mine," Jacob agreed. "And I can dispose o' it as I choose. If I choose to give to yeh, what's ta stop me?"

Dave crossed his arms, and said, "Naught but my pride. I'll not accept it thusly."

"I'll trade it to yeh then," declared Jacob.

"Trade it?" Jacob could tell this was something Dave would consider. "What would yeh trade it for?"

Jacob had noticed a finely crafted tomahawk hanging at the Virginian's belt. "I'll trade it for yer tomahawk."

The Virginian's hand went to his tomahawk. He eyed Jacob with a mixture of belligerence and respect. "By Jamie, yeh know where to strike a man, don't yeh? I had ta go all the way to North Carolina for this blade." His face mellowed. "Aw hell, I was plannin' ta visit North Carolina agin anyway." He grinned. "I got a sister in them parts. I can replace it." And he drew his tomahawk, and offered it to Jacob. "Yeh've a deal ifn yeh mean it."

Jacob was happy to take the tomahawk in his left hand, and Dave's hand in his right. The trade was done. But Jacob believed he had gained more than a tomahawk and a yoke of oxen; he had gained a friend in the lanky Virginian. "Perhaps we'll meet again," he said.

He was rewarded by a grin from Dave. "Yeh never can tell."

17 Miranda's Warrant

December, 1770

The Sunday after the shooting match, Jacob was seated with his brother across from Mr. Wallace and Hannah's father in the O'Malley parlor. They were awaiting the dinner at which Mr. O'Malley would announce Jacob's betrothal to Hannah.

Hannah's little sister, Sarah, ran in crying, "Papa, a rider is coming; riding fast."

Mr. O'Malley leaped up and, grabbing his rifle from its place over the mantle, strode to the porch followed by the three others. True enough, a rider was pounding down the road toward them.

At first Jacob thought it was Mr. Sablonski; it looked like him, but he then noticed the rider had red hair, and realized he was Dick, Mr. Sablonski's son. He had not seen Dick since he had left Wynnewood. "It is Dick Sablonski," he told the rest, and went to meet him.

Dick pulled his horse to a sliding stop, and leaped to the ground. Before Jacob could greet him, he cried in German, "You must flee, Jacob. Miranda's discovered your whereabouts, and she's gotten the magistrate to swear out a warrant for your arrest.

My father told me to look for you here first. Thank God I have found you."

"But . . . but . . ." Jacob could not take it in. "Why would the magistrate swear out a warrant? He ruled the death was an accident."

"There is a new magistrate," Dick said desperately.

"How did she find I am here?"

"The match you won the other day--you were recognized, and your name is known everywhere." Dick grabbed Jacob, and shoved him toward the porch. "I tell you, you must flee. She has sent men to capture you. They cannot be far behind." When Jacob stopped, and turned to face him, he grabbed Jacob by both shoulders. "If they capture you, you'll be hung for sure."

He glanced at the men on the porch, and switched to English. "Yeh must help him flee. His life is in danger."

"In danger?" Mr. O'Malley asked. He stepped from the porch cradling his rifle, and stared at Jacob. "What does this mean, Jacob?"

How can I possibly explain? wondered Jacob, but Dick blurted out, "He has a warrant on his head for murder."

"Murder!"

"It is my fault," cried Mateo.

"No," yelled Jacob. When Mateo began to again speak he ordered him in German. "Don't you say another word. Not to anyone."

He switched to English, and addressed Mr. O'Malley. "It is something that happened before I came here." He regarded them in despair. How could he make them understand?

Dick said urgently. "We do not have time to explain the particulars, he must flee."

Mr. Wallace stepped forward, and declared, "Ah have nae need ta hear the particulars. Ah shall never believe him to be guilty."

"No more shall I," said Mr. O'Malley, and he hustled everyone into the house, and sent his daughter Sarah to take Dick's horse into the barn.

"Luella," he ordered his wife, "Pack bread and whatever else Jacob could easily carry into a pack. Rachel, help her." The two ran to obey.

Mr. O'Malley then thrust his rifle into Jacob's hand, went to the shelf where he kept his powder and shot, made sure they were full, and handed them to Jacob. "Yeh'll take my rifle." When Jacob tried to protest, he stopped him with a look. "Yeh'll take my rifle."

He went into his back room, and Jacob looked to where Hannah stood staring at him. He had never before seen fear in her eyes; she was afraid now. He handed the rifle, bag, and horn to his brother, and turned to her only to find she had come to him.

She was in his arms with her face buried in his shoulder. He caressed the back of her head, and drank in the sweet odor of her hair.

What can I say to her?

"Jacob, oh Jacob." She lifted her face to him. He saw it was now wet with tears. "I don't know what I shall do if yeh are captured."

"I shall not be captured."

How can I promise that?

"Where shall yeh go?"

Where? He did not know. "To the Kishacoquillas Valley," he heard himself say. *Yes, I'll go there.* "Surely they shall lose my trail long before then." He forced himself to grin. "This shall be my opportunity to scout out a good site for our farm."

She tried to return his smile, but failed. He lifted her face to his own, and kissed her.

He heard her father returning, and released her.

"I shall love yeh forever," she whispered. She shoved him away. "Now go."

She ran from the room just as her father returned with a blanket, a coat, and a knife, and Rachel entered with a bag of food. The knife Mr. O'Malley held out to Jacob who stuck it into his belt, and the food and coat he rolled tightly in the blanket and tied them with a short rope leaving a loop so Jacob could strap it upon his back. Finally he reached within his coat, and withdrew a small bag of coins which he held out to Jacob.

"I'll not take yer money, Mr. O'Malley."

"Yeh have no idea what lays before yeh, son," Mr. O'Malley said. "Yeh may need it more than I," and he pressed it into Jacob's hand.

"Aye," Jacob heard his master say. The bag was snatched away, and his master poured more coins into it before returning it. "D'na argue, but go."

The men urged Jacob to the back door. At the door Jacob turned to Mr. O'Malley. "I . . . I'll leave yer rifle at the Gerbers. Yeh may fetch it there."

"Just take it, Jacob. A rifle can be replaced; a life cannot."

"I'll be getting my own rifle."

"But the men pursuing yeh," cried Dick. "I tell yeh they are not far behind me."

"I'll be getting my own rifle," Jacob said stubbornly. "Besides, the Gerbers are on my way north."

"Then be on yer way," urged Mr. O'Malley. He hurried Jacob through the door. "And Jacob," he said quietly. "Yeh'll return for Hannah when yeh may."

"But . . ."

"Yeh'll return for her when yeh may," he repeated firmly. "Naught has changed betwixt us." He shoved him down the steps.

Jacob stared through the doorway to where Hannah stood wide eyed. He wanted to go to her, but she cried, "Run, Jacob. Run."

He ran.

Mateo followed him. "I'm coming with you."

Jacob nodded and, without another word, led his brother on a fast run to the tree lot where they turned to race to the Gerbers. Jacob remembered Woosamequin's teaching that a man can cover ground quicker and longer with a fast lope instead of a run and adjusted their pace.

Fortunately the Gerbers were yet at their church gathering. The Amish met together only every other Sunday, but when they did, they spent the entire day fellowshipping. Jacob was relieved they were not home for he had neither the time nor desire to bid them goodbye and explain his reasons for leaving.

Jacob left Mr. O'Malley's rifle on their bed, gathered his own rifle, Dave's tomahawk, and a few other things, and ran to the north edge of the farm before stopping to address Mateo.

"This is as far as you shall go."

Mateo glared at him. "I am coming with you."

"No. You are not." He stared at his defiant brother standing before him, and lay his rifle carefully down and dropped his pack at his feet before taking him by the shoulders. "Don't you understand? If I am caught they shall hang me. If you are with me they shall hang you too."

He watched his brother wrestle with his emotions for a moment before mastering them and saying, "If they hang you, they shall have to hang me too. I will want to hang with you."

"But I do NOT want you to hang with me." Jacob shook him angrily. "I want you to live! You must live."

Mateo threw his arms around Jacob, and buried his face into his shoulder. "But I'm the one who killed the fat bastard. You should not have to die when it is my fault."

Jacob sank to his knees, and peered up into his brother's eyes. "Never say that again," he ordered harshly. "It was not your fault." He stared at him for several moments. "You saved my life. Even if they hang me tomorrow, I shall have lived three years longer than I would if it had not been for you."

He forced himself to grin. "But I do not intend to allow them to hang me."

Mateo did not smile. "I want to come with you."

"You cannot."

Mateo's face dissolved, and he buried it into his hands as he sank to the ground and wailed, "Do not leave me, Jacob. I don't want to stay here without you." His body shook with sobs, and he lifted a tearful face to his brother. "Please take me with you."

Jacob took him into his arms, and rocked him as if he were a small child. After several moments he said, "I love you too much to take you with me, Mateo. Mr. Sablonski has told me Miranda has never mentioned you. She only seeks me. She has forgotten about you. I do not want her to be reminded."

He lifted Mateo's face, and forced him to look at him. "I want you to stay here with the Gerbers. Lots of people hereabouts know you're my brother, but they'll not betray you. You shall be safe."

Mateo's face hardened. "If you leave me, I shall follow you."

Jacob knew he could; Mateo had learned Woosamequin's lessons very well.

"You know that would be very dangerous, Mateo, not only for you, but for me. You know two trails are far easier to follow than one."

Mateo's eyes did not waver. Jacob considered for a moment; how could he prevent him from following?

"Listen to me, Mateo. I am your brother, and I know what is best for you. I want you to promise me you shall remain here with the Gerbers for six months." He paused. "If I am still free after six months, I shall send word through the Indians to Woosamequin where you may find me. If at that time you think I was wrong, and you still wish to follow me, you may."

He stared Mateo in the eye. "But I want you to swear you shall wait six months."

Mateo glared at him for several long moments before he finally nodded, but Jacob insisted, "Say it. Swear to it."

Mateo's eyes were still very hard but he said, "I swear I shall remain with the Gerbers for six months." Then he leaped to his feet, and ran back to the Gerber barn.

Jacob watched him go, and then sadly gathered his pack and his gun, turned his back upon his brother, and began his flight.

End of book two: Jacob's Youth

The author very much hopes you have enjoyed the first two books of Jacob's Struggles. If you have comments or suggestions, he would love to hear from you at:

> Kinderi Publishing
> 2101 East M36
> Pinckney, Mi 48169

The first chapter of *Jacob's Exile*, the third book of *Jacob's Struggles.* has been included for your reading pleasure. Enjoy!

1   Exile

April, 1771

Jacob lay shivering in the dark abandoned cabin.

How long have I been running?

It had been weeks certainly, maybe months since the horrible day when the men had come from Wynnewood to arrest him for the murder of his old master. The time since had been one long miserable blur of narrow escapes. At least he had been spared an adventure the past few days.

Maybe I've finally lost 'em.

He refused to believe it; he had been disappointed before. He shifted his weight trying to find a comfortable position. The day he had spent huddled in a pine tree watching for pursuers had been miserable, but he believed he preferred it to the horrid darkness spent lying on a hard dirt floor.

At least I'm out of the wind.

The cabin was ideal, for it had a hole in the rear wall, and was built into a stand of pines which would conceal his escape if he had to use it. He would not have dared spend the night in the cabin if it had not. He knew he should be thankful he had found the cabin. But he did wish he dared to light a fire; he was so cold.

He could not help wishing he were sleeping warm and safe beside his brother and rejoicing in his betrothal to Hannah.

Why, oh why, did those men have to discover my whereabouts the very day her father was to give her to me?

He had not killed the old brute; Mateo, his brother, had, but no one knew that but the two brothers and Jacob had made Mateo swear he would never reveal it. Jacob would far rather die than see his brother die. Besides, Mateo had only killed their master to prevent him killing Jacob. But since both Jacob and Mateo had been indentured, they had known they would have to flee. For so many wonderful years they had evaded detection; they had thought themselves safe.

He wondered how long it would be before it would be safe for him to return to his brother and Hannah. He knew it could be a very long time.

When he had been first forced to flee, he had assumed he would simply have to evade the men Miranda, his old master's daughter, had sent from Wynnewood.

He chuckled to remember how easily he had lost them.

But he had very soon discovered she had, in addition to sending those men, caused fliers to be sent everywhere with a reward on his head . . . a large reward. He had never realized before how much power money wielded. It seemed everyone in the entire colony was on his trail seeking that reward.

I don't even know where I am anymore; it's been days since I've seen a settlement.

He struggled not to despair, and felt self pity rise to engulf him.

Why must I be separated from all I love . . . again? Why did God allow this to happen to me?

But he remembered the words of Job: 'Shall I accept blessings from the Lord but not adversity?'

And he felt the small book of Psalms which he had found tucked with the food Mrs. O'Malley had provided for his escape. When he had first found it, he had been tempted to toss it aside; of what use was a book of Psalms in his dilemma? It only took up valuable space and added weight. But he had kept it and read from it when he could. It had been more comfort than he could have dreamed. More than once he had blessed Mrs. O'Malley for her foresight and generosity in giving it to him.

He wished he had light enough to read from it now.

David the King was pursued as I am, with even less justification, yet in the end God delivered him. I must trust he shall deliver me.

He remembered his grandfather saying, "You never know what God has planned for your future; the important thing is to survive." He grinned wryly. *What if you have naught but misery in your future?*

But he remembered asking that question of himself on the long cold nights in his master's barn when he had felt like giving up the struggle. Then he could not have imagined a brother like Mateo or friends like Mr. Wallace, Mr. O'Malley, or the Gerbers, much less a gal like Hannah. How much he would have missed had he not survived and persevered. His old grandfather had been right after all.

He froze, his contemplations interrupted. He knew not what was amiss, but his senses had detected danger. He rolled out of his blanket, took up his rifle, and crawled to the chink low in the front wall. That was another fortuitous aspect of the cabin he had noticed; it enabled him to see outside without revealing himself.

He saw two, no, three, men creeping toward the cabin. Who were they? Were they pursuers or strangers who meant him no harm? The fact that they seemed to be stalking toward the cabin was an ominous sign, but he needed to know with what type of men he was dealing.

One was briefly revealed by the faint moonlight. His head was bald except for a ridge of hair running across his scalp from front to back. They were Iroquois!

All of the lurid bloody tales he had been told of the Iroquois rose up before Jacob and he scurried as fast as he could to his escape hole, and squeezed through. He had left his blanket and other provisions behind, but it could not be helped. Only escape mattered now.

He slipped as quickly yet noiselessly through the pines as he could knowing it would be but moments before the fiends would be on his trail, and then he ran trying to remember all of the tricks for throwing pursuers off one's trail.

God in heaven, have I not enough men seeking my blood? Why must these vipers seek it as well? Please help me escape.

He did not wish to die.

At least white men would have killed me quickly and mercifully had they captured me. Have I gone through all my troubles and misery to elude them only to face a horrid tortuous death at the hand of these fiends?

He ran harder.

* * * *

Jacob glanced at the sun. It had risen, crawled excruciatingly across the sky, and was finally low on the horizon. Still his pursuers followed, and still Jacob fled. Yet he began to allow himself to hope.

If I can remain free until dark, I may yet escape them.

But he was so weary and hungry.

Shall I ever reach the crest of this hill?

It seemed he had been climbing forever but he had had no choice for the Iroquois were both to his left and right as well as behind. It took all he had just to keep ahead of them.

Finally the ground leveled off, and he increased his speed; if he could just put a little distance between himself and the fiends pursuing him . . .

He burst from the trees, and skidded to a stop in horror. Before him was a vast void.

He looked over the cliff at the ground far below, at least a hundred feet he guessed. He saw no path down. He nearly collapsed in despair. It was over. It was only a matter of minutes before the Iroquois would be upon him; he had no escape.

Then he noticed a great oak tree growing at the base of the cliff; its upper branches were a mere twenty feet or so below the cliff edge. Throwing caution aside, Jacob ran and leaped.

For horrifying seconds he fell, and then crashed into the green canopy of the oak. Limbs snapped and broke as they clawed, scrapped, and pummeled him. But Jacob kept his arms and legs close to his body, forced himself to remain limp, and trusted the limbs to slow his descent. He knew the best way to avoid a broken bone was to remain limber, and he did not wish to have an extremity snagged and wrenched from him.

He bounced from limb to limb like a great ball, but his speed was slowing.

He finally ventured to grab at a pliable branch. It bowed, and swung him toward the center of the tree. Too late he saw a huge branch in his path; he and it collided with a horrible blow, but he grabbed hold and clung to it. His ribs screamed, and he could not breathe, but he was finally stopped. Trying not to moan, he struggled atop the branch, and lay.

After a moment he surveyed his aching body. He found that although he had received a good many bruises, he had broken no bones. Ignoring his body's objections, he moved further into the tree's foliage, and concealed himself from the cliff top.

He waited.

Is it more dangerous to move while there may be someone on the cliff to observe me, or to remain here while they find a path down the cliff?

He did not know.

He saw that the branches of the tree intertwined with those of a tree to its left and he worked his way to them, leaped into the next tree and then into a third. That had been one of Mateo's favorite tricks, and a successful one. The sun had lowered enough that the base of the cliff was in shadow; he needed to find a way out of the tiny valley he was in while he could still see, or find a place to hide.

His eye fell upon a great fallen tree. He could see midway along it a large hollow filled with leaves and other vegetative debris. He resolved to attempt to gain that hollow and conceal himself therein. With little difficulty he did so. He congratulated himself that he had left no trail from the oak into which he had cast himself to the log.

He worked himself and his rifle into the debris trying hard to leave no trace. The dead leaves and other vegetation were damp and very odorous, but he found their decay was generating a very pleasant heat. For the first time in weeks, he was warm.

And he was soon asleep.

www.ingramcontent.com/pod-product-compliance
Lightning Source LLC
Chambersburg PA
CBHW070836120626
46556CB00002B/780